hope burned

NATE, NICOLE & FAMILY:
I AM SO HONORED TO BE
A PART OF SUCH A GREAT
FAMILY. JUST BEING AROUND
YOU ALL FOR ONE WEEK
MAKES ME STRIVE TO BE
A BETTER HUSBAND, FATHER
AND IN TURN, PERSON.
    THANK YOU FOR WELCOMING
ME INTO YOUR LIVES.
    THANKING YOU ALWAYS,

        BRENT.
        2011

hope burned

BRENT LAPORTE

MISFIT

ECW

Published by ECW Press
2120 Queen Street East, Suite 200
Toronto, Ontario, Canada M4E 1E2
416.694.3348 / info@ecwpress.com

LIBRARY AND ARCHIVES CANADA CATALOGUING IN PUBLICATION

LaPorte, Brent
Hope burned / Brent LaPorte.

"A misFit book"
ISBN 978-1-55022-963-9

1. Title.

PS8623.A7368H66 2010   C813'.6   C2010-901260-7

Cover Photo and Design: Bill Douglas at The Bang
Text Design: Melissa Kaita
Typesetting: Mary Bowness
Editor: Michael Holmes / a misFit book
Printing: Coach House Printing   2   3   4   5

This book is set in Adobe Garamond Pro.

The publication of *Hope Burned* has been generously supported by the Canada Council for the Arts which last year invested $20.1 million in writing and publishing throughout Canada, by the Ontario Arts Council, by the Government of Ontario through Ontario Book Publishing Tax Credit, by the OMDC Book Fund, an initiative of the Ontario Media Development Corporation, and by the Government of Canada through the Canada Book Fund.

ONTARIO ARTS COUNCIL
CONSEIL DES ARTS DE L'ONTARIO   Canada   Canada Council   Conseil des Arts
for the Arts   du Canada

PRINTED AND BOUND IN CANADA

ECW PRESS
ecwpress.com

for Suzie,
with love

. . . there's nothin' strange
About an axe with bloodstains in the barn

There's always some killin'
You got to do around the farm

—Tom Waits

I'M NOT REALLY MUCH of a letter writer, but I felt it was important to explain to you exactly why, today, I killed both my father and grandfather.

Not exactly your typical "How are things?" is it?

For that, I apologize.

For the killings I do not.

I suppose, like any good story, I should begin at the start, or start at the beginning, whichever you choose. I'm honestly not sure just how it all began, how old I am or even *who* I am. I do know, however, exactly where I came from, where I am now and how I got here.

This is what I will try to explain to you.

If you want to understand where I'm from simply Google "scary desolate farm property." A picture of the family house will pop up immediately. I say *house* and not *home* intentionally. A house is a place where a person lives. A home is a place where a person is alive. There is a difference.

While I lived in this house, I was never truly alive.

Being alive means you're capable of making a choice and have some sort of effect on your surroundings— you can appreciate the wind, the trees, the grass. . . . Any of God's gifts are present every time you open your eyes. When you're alive you choose to take deep breaths on your own. Simply existing means being able to breathe only because someone else has allowed you to take a breath.

Alive can be defined as a form of awakening: becoming aware of your surroundings for the first time and being able to appreciate all their benefits. When you're alive you can choose to order cheese on the burger. Fries? Yes or no? Living means you eat whatever slop is thrown at you. Being alive means that you can choose to lower the shades to darken a room so you can sleep late; living is counting the minutes until someone opens the trapdoor to let a small sliver of light into your dungeon so you can see what's been crawling over you all night.

You may not want to know, but you need to. If for no other reason than to make your nightmares complete.

Yes, my young man, there is a difference between living and being alive. Fortunately, you will never have to experience this. From the moment you were born, you were alive—awakened, aware and, yes, even aroused within your surroundings. I suppose it is because of the depravation I suffered that I appreciate the difference.

This house? It is a very desolate place, not likely to welcome others for very many years. Well off the main highways, hidden by the forests: out of sight, out of mind.

My grandfather owned all of the property around here: roads, forests, the lake and yes, for a period of time, even me. Everything was hidden, kept from the outside world.

How he came to own this property I still do not know, although I suspect it was left to him by a more ambitious ancestor.

It is a typical farmhouse of an era long past, when it was not unusual for a family to exceed ten in numbers. This table that I am now sitting at for the first time, writing this letter, seats fourteen. In all likelihood it was constructed of the ancestors of the forest that have kept this place hidden all of these years. If only they knew what they would become, maybe they would have chosen to submit to the forest floor instead of shooting skywards.

As I write this I look around the large country kitchen and try to imagine the room full of the type of warmth that only a country family could provide. I try to wipe the horror of earlier from my mind with visions of children laughing, men playing fiddle and ladies dancing. But it doesn't work. The kitchen is too dark, the smoke-stained walls too constricting, the tobacco-stained floor too dirty.

I am gazing at a photo of my great-grandparents. The oval-shaped frame houses a dark-eyed, lifeless-looking man. His gaze bores right through the unfortunate photographer. His thin lips show not even a hint of a smile. His skin, cured by the sun, is beginning to sag under his chin. He appears tall and thin, like most men of his day. Men beaten down by the very thing they loved: farming.

The woman next to him has dark-centered eyes, but they're light-rimmed, green or hazel. While his eyes look through the photographer, hers are looking into him, to his core, his soul. Knowing his every thought, his every want, his every fear. I feel vulnerable still.

She does not appear to be an overly large woman, nor does she appear to be small. I suppose the term to use would be stout. Very capable of handling her chores on what had been a working farm. No doubt she could bake a pie one minute and birth a calf the next. Her silver hair is pulled back into a no-nonsense type of bun, exposing oversized ears and a full neck and face. Her mouth is closed to a point, giving the impression that she could fire arrows through it, striking a man through the heart should he step out of line. From all appearances, she likely did.

That, my son, is all I have for your family tree. Other than my father and grandfather, of course.

The photos that hang in this kitchen are all I knew

of other humans for most of my stay at the farm. I say *most* because on one occasion I did catch a glimpse of life outside.

I had just finished in the potato field for the day and was making my way back to the house for bed when I heard the sound of my grandfather's old truck rumbling down the dirt road. Now, I will tell you that I was never before, nor again, left outside when my father knew Grandpa was returning from his monthly trip to town.

It was one of those mid-summer days when even grasshoppers and ants are lazy. Nothing was moving particularly fast, especially not my father. I had just rounded the house when my grandfather parked his faded red pickup just outside the mill by the lake. I kind of half-hid at the side of the house while he got out of the driver's door and hurried to the passenger side. I didn't know why I was hiding; I just was. At that point I knew I didn't want to be seen. I watched as my grandpa flung the door open and pulled out a young girl, likely twelve or thirteen. He had her firmly by the arm, even though she was not resisting.

Keep in mind I had never seen, to my recollection, a living human being other than my father and grandfather at this point in my life. A wave of emotion shook through me. I thought, *My God, there are others out there.* I was shaken by the beauty of the creature my grandfather was leading towards the mill.

She had the most beautiful long blond hair, and skin that appeared smoother than anything I had ever seen or touched. She was wearing a brown flowered sundress; one of the straps was broken and lying loosely over her shoulder. The dress swayed in the summer breeze. In any other setting it would have been the picture of a beautiful girl about to enjoy a perfect summer day down by the lake with family. Unfortunately, this was not any other setting. She was not going for a picnic of fried chicken and salad, topped off with ice-cold lemonade. This girl was about to see the sun for the last time. She would never feel the wind caress her skin, blowing her hair about her face, again.

The dry August leaves were rustling and the swaying branches were groaning for water when she looked up over the shoulder with the broken strap and spotted me. To this day I do not know how she knew I was standing there, but she looked over and straight into my heart. Her dark eyes did not plead for help, nor were they angry, but they were not empty or lifeless. They were dark pools of resignation—shimmering with despair. My grandpa led her a few steps farther and then noticed her staring at me.

He glared at me with his own large dark eyes. There was no other emotion but anger and hatred. He said nothing, just grabbed the girl by the arm, almost yanking it out of its socket. He led her like that to the mill, and outside of my dreams I never saw her again.

That night my grandfather came into the farmhouse as I was preparing dinner. He was covered in sweat, hair tangled, with fresh scratches on his face and arms. She did not give up as easily as he would have liked. He had his pound of flesh, no doubt, but she also had hers. He walked into the kitchen with his shirt torn open; his studded leather belt was in one hand, and he held his pants up with the other. If I didn't know what was coming, I would have found it comical. The studs of the belt would leave huge welts on my back and buttocks. He never said a word; his eyes did all of the talking. The first swat caught me just below my right ear and cut my throat enough to scare but not kill me. As I hit the floor, lash after lash fell on my back. He had never hit me with such ferocity before. Normally my back would go numb about halfway through such a beating, but this time the last strike hurt every bit as much as the first. My blood pooled. I could not even crawl away; the floor was too greasy from the blood. All I could do was lie there and take more. I remember thinking this might be the time that I did not make it. Now, most kids my age would have been terrified at the sight of so much of their own blood. Hell, most kids are terrified at a nosebleed. Not me. I would guess there isn't an inch of floor in this old house that doesn't have traces of my blood on it.

The interval between the strikes became longer as

the old man's strength ebbed. I just lay there because if I showed any resistance, or tried to move away, he would have been reinvigorated. Finally he exhausted himself and left me, sobbing and hoping to die. It was then that my father, who was likely waiting for the beating to end, came into the house. He paused, looked at the old man, then grabbed me by the hair and dragged me to my crawlspace. He'd done this many times before, but the lubricated floor made the task easier. He threw me down the stairs and I didn't have the strength to break the fall with my hands. I hit every step on the way down and my face was cut wide open. Every inch of my body ached; it hurt to even open my eyes. Somehow I was able to crawl to my bed, and then I collapsed. I had to sleep on my stomach for many days after this. I did not understand, then, that I was being punished for the sins of my family.

NOW, AS ODD AS THIS may sound, my life in this place was relatively typical. Days started out the same, each and every one of them. I would wake to my father's footsteps on the floor above. He would make his way to the door of the crawlspace pretty much as any father might wake his child for school. The difference, of course, was his tone, and the language he used to rouse me. I never got a gentle rub of the forehead, a tousle of my hair or a whispered, "It's time to get up."

If I wasn't already awake I heard, "Get your goddamned lazy ass up here and start that fire."

He would then shuffle off to relieve himself—a luxury I would have to wait for until after the fire was lit.

One morning—I suppose it must have been in the fall because there were no leaves on the trees and it was damp and cold, even outside of the crawlspace—the firewood was green, and it was a struggle to light the stove. Black smoke billowed as I tried to fan flames to life.

My father sat on a chair in the corner glaring at me as my grandfather made his way to the kitchen. The sound of his boots on the wood floor announced both his arrival and his displeasure with the smoke and the lack of the means to cook his breakfast. I knew I was in for another beating.

Even as the sound neared I dared not look to see his approach. I kept fanning that reluctant wood, trying to will it to ignite so I could escape the consequences of displeasing them. I never felt the blow to the back of my head. When I awoke I could tell that a fire poker had been used to strike because it was lying on the floor near me with my hair and dried blood still on it.

I tried to stand but fell back down almost immediately. Neither my father nor my grandfather offered assistance. My vision was blurred but I could see my grandfather seated in the chair once occupied by my father and my father now standing at the stove.

I remained motionless for a moment and tried to get my bearings, watching as my father took some of the sizzling bacon from the pan and placed it on a plate. God, it smelled good. The bacon smell filled my nostrils, electrifying my taste buds, awakening me to the point that all but my pain sensors were functioning.

I don't know if it was the blow to the head or simply the temptation of the bacon, but for the first time in memory I asked my father for something.

"Pa, that sure smells so good. Do you think I could have some?"

To anyone else in the world I would have been one sorry-looking kid: lying there in dirty overalls, skinny, pale, with blood coming from the back of my head. But to these two?

My father looked at me, then at my grandfather, and said, "It sure does smell good, boy. You want some?" He shifted his look from his pa to me, then back to his pa. "What do you say, Pa, maybe we been a little hard on him? How 'bout we give him . . . just a little?"

I never really caught on to the wickedness of his grin; I was just lying there, hoping that he would finally give me some food that wasn't half-eaten and cold.

My grandfather looked up, spat tobacco on the floor and nodded his head.

My father, the man who made me, looked at the

pan, three-quarters full of sizzling bacon, and said, "Okay, boy, you want some; here it is." And then he dumped the contents of the pan, grease and all, all over me. Mercifully I was able to duck. Most of the liquid fire rolled down my back to leave a trail of burnt flesh in its wake. I suppose the most pathetic aspect of this is that even with my own flesh bubbling from the bacon lava, I still tried to shove as much in my mouth as I could.

Son, it tasted even better than it smelled.

It took at least a week for the boils in my mouth to heal, probably a week more for my back. The mental scars took much longer—though I'm not sure they ever really have.

My nights were spent in the crawlspace. As I've said, I never ate with them; they let me feed off their scraps when they were done with meals. Once in a while, I would gnaw on a raw potato, carrot or whatever other vegetable might be in season. I did have to be careful, however; if they caught me, I would be taught another lesson.

When they weren't watching over me in the fields, they were in the old mill. They still beat me at the end of most days, regardless. It got to the point that I wasn't scared of getting caught sneaking food because I was going to suffer anyway. I would stuff all the dirty vegetables I could into my mouth; it didn't make a difference.

Originally my bed was the same dirt that kept the vegetables cool and supported the foundation. After my many childhood illnesses they realized I needed something more suitable to a human being. If, in fact, that's what I was. I was no good to them when I was sick. It was only when I was physically incapable of moving that I was relieved of my duties.

This was not without its own degradation.

"Oh look, Pa, poor boy's limping. He can't start the stove. Says his ribs are sore, can't hardly breathe. Poor soulless sonofabitch."

Talk like that usually led to another kick to the ribs or groin—or my head, if I happened to be on my knees.

As I've told you with this letter, I was a slave to my father and his father. What I haven't told you is my father was also a slave to his father.

It is both difficult and easy to explain the power a father has over his own son. At five you may defy me, but you will never cease to believe me—or believe in me. You don't bat an eye when I talk about Santa Claus, the Easter Bunny or Tooth Fairy. In fact you want me to go further with those stories; you want to believe. Hell, you should—you should want to believe. You should want to believe your father.

I never believed in mine.

Unfortunately, like you, he believed in his.

I suppose that the main difference between him

and me is that I could never understand how he could sit there and let his own father beat his son.

My grandfather used to go to town every five or six weeks to sell vegetables. I used to help them pack that pickup with all the potatoes, cabbage, red beets, lettuce and whatever else it would hold. He would drive down that old road—a road I was forbidden to walk upon—and disappear for four or five days. I wouldn't see him and for that I was glad, for I have never in my life met a more selfish, despicable, evil man. And yes, I should add, I have met some pretty bad men in my adult life.

Contrary to what a sane person might expect, once my grandfather left, my father's temperament actually grew worse.

Someone normal (if such a being exists) might actually expect my father to have eased my suffering in the absence of his own tormentor. No, my father sought ways to increase the pain, to turn up the pressure, to deepen my degradation.

I suppose the most humiliation I have ever felt, and there's been so much, was one time shortly after my grandfather had left on one of his excursions. I was tending to one of the gardens and after the smell of the old truck's exhaust had cleared, my father approached. He stood there in his dirty overalls, reeking of whiskey, his body swaying in the breeze—partly because of the uneven ground, but mostly because of the booze. I kept working, pretending he wasn't there, hoping that if I ignored him long enough he would leave. I knew by his stance that this wouldn't be the case.

"You like it here?"

"Yes, sir," I said, already afraid of where this might lead.

"Why don't you get up outta that dirt and get back to the house and fix up some dinner. It's getting cold and we're gonna need a fire tonight."

"Yes, sir."

I stood up and approached gingerly, the same way a wild animal approaches the open hand of a human. The need to taste the food from the hand overrides the fear. He must have sensed this because as we walked back to the house he paused and looked at me with his yellow-green eyes and gave me what appeared to be a genuine smile. His eyes flashed from threatening to something almost trustworthy. In retrospect, I am sure this is the same smile that many have seen while drinking with my father, just before he broke a pool cue over their head. Nonetheless, for some reason, I needed to trust him.

I was preparing the stove for the fire when he spoke again. "Son, you can tell me. You ever thought about runnin' away to the city? I mean, yer grandpa ain't the most kind-hearted person. Shit, he can be a downright nasty ornery sonofabitch." He was drinking straight from the bottle, eyeing me for any reaction. I believed it was a trap and tried my best to lie. I was just starting to heal from the last beating and was in no rush for another.

"Grandpa's fine. He lets me sleep in the crawlspace, gave me his old mattress and blankets. Why would I want to leave?"

"C'mon boy, you can tell yer ol' man. Tell you the truth, I been thinkin' 'bout leavin' the old prick myself. Been getting a little too ornery with me, an' I don't like much how he been treatin' you." He leaned the chair back on its hind legs and ran his fingers through his straw-colored hair to give the impression that he was putting some thought into this, some sort of sincerity, like a man trying to solve a math problem.

I guess I felt I could trust him then—I mean he was right about Grandpa being more ornery. I had never heard him like this before. Truthfully, I had never thought about leaving. And to be honest, I never knew "the city" even existed. I guess I should have known that there were other places, I just never allowed myself to consider it.

"Is there somewheres else we could go, Pa?"

Smile, lips closed; eyes narrow, slits now—satisfied he had a nibble on his line.

"Sure there is." He was drinking even more heavily, and seemed content to humor me; otherwise, I would have already been in my dungeon.

"Son, you ever hear of Nashville? Or Las Vegas or

New York City?"

He knew I hadn't.

"No, sir."

His face took on a new air of superiority. I mean, he always looked down on me, but this was something else. I suppose it's the same look most dads get when they first show their son how to throw a curve, ride a bike or dive off a cliff—but my dad's big moment in the sun was telling me that other people actually existed. Quite a revelation.

"Nashville," he said, "is the birthplace of country music. All the great stars play there. Dolly Parton, Kenny Rogers, Tanya Tucker, George Jones and my personal favorite, Miss Loretta Lynn." He paused to light a cigarette, exhaled and continued. "A coal miner's daughter. Yes, sir, that woman come from nuthin'. Dirt, dust and shit. Goddamned can she sing, though. Like an angel. What a voice. Raised not much different than you—turned her into a damned millionaire." He wasn't looking at me then, he was seeing something I could neither imagine nor comprehend. And then he lost that dreamy look we all get when we are reminiscing, his face becoming rigid, jaw taut, angry. It lasted for just a moment and then he was brought back to where he was, what he was doing.

"Did you know, son, Loretta Lynn never cooks for herself? She don't clean, sweep, light a fire. . . . Hell, I'm surprised she even wipes her own ass. She shits in a gold toilet. You imagine that? A gold toilet—inside the house. She don't have to put on her boots and go outside to a spider-crawlin', shit-stinkin' outhouse like us poor folk. And why? Well, I'll tell ya. 'Cause she is rich. Filthy fuckin' rich. More money 'an brains." He took another long haul from the jug, paused to let the liquid burn his throat all the way down.

"She don't waste her time picking potatoes, tomatoes or whatever the fuck the old man thinks we should shove into the ground. Hey boy, wouldn't it be nice to shower in hot water instead of washin' the dirt off yer balls in that ol' wash tub once a month? How would you like a bathroom with a sink to wash yer hands after wiping yer ass? I bet Loretta Lynn don't got shit on her hands. No, sir, I imagine she washes 'em off on some goddamned gold-plated sink with gold-plated taps. Probably uses gold soap. Can you imagine that, boy? 'Course you can't. You don't even know what gold is, do you? Jesus Christ, you are one stupid sonofabitch."

He took a long drag off his cigarette and sat for a bit, thinking as the smoke billowed from his now silent mouth up around his head and back down to the draft created by the half-open window. The smoke seemed to dance, like the thoughts running through his mind. Going nowhere and everywhere all at once.

"Pa, could we become rich and shit inside the house?" I asked.

"Boy, do you have any idea what it takes to get rich in this world?"

I did not and replied, "No, sir."

"Well, you either got to have very rich parents or grandparents. Do you think you have very rich parents or grandparents?"

"No, sir, I don't." I did not understand what *rich* meant, only that if it meant having warm running water I did not qualify.

"Well, son, do you have some sort of talent that you think is going to make you rich? You know, like being the winner at the International Potato Picking Contest? Maybe the Tomato Polisher of the Year?"

"I suppose I could, sir."

He began laughing, almost spitting his shine across the room. His face glowed bright red. I had never seen him laugh so hard, and I believed I had done something good. For the first time my father was actually happy.

I liked that.

He stopped laughing and took another hard swig from the jug him and Grandpa kept under the kitchen sink. He wiped his mouth with the back of his hand, still smiling.

"Boy, you have no idea, do you?"

"No idea about what, sir?"

"Life, you goofy little prick. Life."

He took another long draw, contemplating what

he had created. How could a boy of my age not understand that people have running water to flush away their shit, wash their clothes and make ice for their afternoon drinks? I will tell you how: no one ever told me.

Everything my father was saying was new to me. I had no knowledge of the world prior to this.

"So, listen, boy, you think me and you should get ourselves rich and fuck off outta this place?"

I was still reticent, not wanting to acknowledge that I did not like working from sunrise to sunset, picking weeds, vegetables and whatever else they thought I should bend over and pick; that I didn't like sleeping in a damp, cold, rat-infested cellar; that I could do without broken ribs, arms, teeth and whatever else they deemed breakable; that I wanted to eat a hot meal that someone hadn't already sunk tobacco-stained teeth into.

"Well, Pa, I like to work, but I do get awful sore some days," I finally managed.

His green eyes lit up, encouraging me to continue.

"I mean if there was somewhere we could go, you and me, and if Grandpa would be okay . . . we could go . . . couldn't we?"

He hauled a final draw off his cigarette, threw the butt on the floor and got out of his chair. Unsteady, he staggered near. One of the straps of his overalls hung from his shoulder and he clumsily pulled it back in place. He turned his back to me and began to speak. "Boy, we could leave. In fact, your old grandpa's got money we could steal. Shit, the old prick wouldn't even notice if we took a handful." He paused. "You wanna see it?"

I had never seen money before.

"Yes, sir. I sure would."

"Okay, boy, throw some more on that fire. The old man ain't here to bitch 'bout it bein' too hot or us wastin' the fuckin' wood. Pile 'er on, boy. Hell, maybe you'll even feel some heat down there tonight."

I did as he told me. I picked a couple of the biggest logs that would hopefully burn all night and take some of the dampness out of the crawlspace.

He grabbed the jug and said, "Come with me."

We walked down the dark hall towards the bedrooms. The doors were closed and, as I soon found out, locked. My father stopped halfway down the hall, reached up to the top of the doorframe and took down a key.

The floor creaked beneath us. It was strange being on this side of the creaking. I was beginning to get uncomfortable, and then we stopped. Pa fumbled with the key to the lock of my grandfather's door, but finally got it to open.

The room was dark so my father struck a match. Shadows danced. They were like ghosts trying not to be seen, crawling around corners, up the walls, over and under the furniture, dancing with my father as he lit the oil lamp. Then they suddenly disappeared, as though they were as afraid of the light as we are of the dark. The room grew lighter, but not brighter. I don't think there is a light in the world that could brighten that place. The four-post pine bed was unmade, sheets and blankets hanging about as though they were trying to strangle it. They were discolored, likely not washed in a year. The smell of my grandfather was everywhere.

Dirty work clothes were thrown in a corner, the pile as high as my waist. I never knew he had more than one set. I honestly didn't.

There were no photos, no indication that the man had personal effects. No jewelry, dress clothes, not even a mirror.

My father led me to a corner of the room where an old rocker sat. He dragged it forward and knelt. He was so unsteady I had to grab him before he toppled.

"Git yer fucking hands offa me, I don' need yer help," he spat. I wasn't sure whether his disgust was with me or with himself.

I couldn't see precisely which floorboards he removed, but I did see the old green strongbox he raised. It was beaten, and no doubt older than my father.

I held the oil lamp as he got to his feet. I followed him to the bed. He straightened one of the dirty blankets and emptied the contents of the box.

Rolls of paper money and coins scattered, but I truthfully had no idea what they were. I had never seen such things before; the coins sparkled with the lamp's flickering.

Other things that fell to the bed were equally puzzling and enticing: ribbons, hair clips, bracelets. Were they valuable? I didn't know.

My father picked up a handful of the silver pieces and said, "Whatta ya think, boy? Sure is pretty, ain't it?"

The light continued to play as he dropped individual coins back onto the bed. I think the silver only became more enticing because of the hideous surroundings.

"Yes, sir; they are pretty." I was mesmerized: I wanted to touch one of them—all of them—hold them, take them and bring them into my crawlspace. Maybe they would carry off the light, ward off the rats that seem so intent on devouring me.

As if he read my thoughts, my father slapped me on the side of the head, grabbed a roll of the paper money and said, "Boy, this is a lesson fer ya. This here rolla paper money ain't real pretty, but just one is worth a whole bag a them there coins. Don' be fooled by pretty things. 'Cause something is pretty, don' make it worth nothing. You understand?"

Actually I did. I'm not sure what prompted him to offer that piece of advice, but it would prove useful.

As quickly as he'd emptied the box, he gathered up the money and trinkets and put them back, careful to replace everything as it was—a quick tousle of the sheets, and we left as quietly as we entered.

We returned to the kitchen without a word, pausing only long enough for my father to return the key to the top of the closet doorframe.

The firewood I'd selected was proving worth its weight. The heat coming off the stove was oppressive. My father swayed back and forth, the full effect of the alcohol enhanced by the boiler-room temperature. He was trying to focus his gaze, but at that point I'm sure he wasn't able to focus on any thing in particular.

"Whatta ya think, boy? Should we rob the old man blind and get the fuck outta this shit hole? Get you some store-bought clothes? Would you like a pair a shoes, boy? How 'bout some nice clean pants?"

I didn't know how to answer.

"Dint you hear, boy? What say we crack the old man over the head with an ax, take the money and his truck and go find Loretta Lynn? Ain't no one gonna miss the ol' bastard. Ain't no one cares 'bout him but us, an' shit, we hate him." He began laughing, so I started to laugh with him.

Finally, I felt comfortable enough to say, "Pa, if you want to, I'll leave with you. I sure would like shoes. My feet do get sore walkin' on rocks and such all day."

"Boy, with the money in there I could buy you a hundred pair." With that, he gestured for me to come closer and began to whisper. Maybe it was the shine, maybe he was getting all choked up, but it seemed like an incredible breakthrough in our relationship. His voice became quieter and I had to get near to make out what he was trying to tell me. He had one hand up on the warming rack over the stove and beckoned me with the other. When I was next to him he pulled me even closer and whispered something unintelligible in my ear.

"What was that, sir?"

He grabbed me by my left ear then, and shoved the right side of my face onto the top of the almost glowing stove. I screamed and tried to pull away while he yelled, "I said if you ever even think of leaving here I will burn the other side of your face, your hands, your feet and your nuts!"

The smell of burning flesh almost made me vomit. The pain from my burnt face and ear did.

I fell to my hands and knees and he kicked me in the ribs. I dry-heaved until I was exhausted.

The old man stood over me. "You'll see that fuckin' mark on yer fuckin' face every time you look in a mirror, boy, and you'll remember. You'll remember who fuckin' owns you—I fuckin' own yer ass. You will never, ever, leave here, understand?"

I couldn't speak. He kicked me again and yelled

even more loudly. "Who owns you? Who owns you, boy? Where you goin', boy? Where you goin'?"

Somehow I managed, "You own me, Pa. I ain't goin' nowhere."

He glared, maybe expecting more of a fight, maybe surprised that I could manage words at all.

I lay there on the floor for God knows how long. Jesus, I had never felt such pain. But what I didn't feel was humiliation. Or defeat. No, despite the agony, I felt hope. Once I knew there was a place to escape to, I also knew that I would get there. I knew I did not have to live like this.

WE'RE SITTING IN THE HOUSE now, you and me. There's still no electricity and I am writing this by the light of an oil lamp. It's summer, so there is no fire for heat, and there's no one to cook for.

They're both dead, yes. My masters are no longer.

It's strange sitting here at the head of this old pine table, writing to you. I suppose, for now, I am the head of this family.

The lamp flickers as though it knows its masters are gone. It fights to die. It whimpers, jumps and tries to hide, to make my task as difficult as possible. But the oil is a greater force and the lamp stays lit. It's the true master. A man can turn a knob and light as many matches as he wants, but without oil, there is no light. The lamp begrudgingly allows me to go on. It's almost as though it does not want me to write to you. But I would write this in the dark if I had to. Because I must.

I look at you lying on the old man's chair. You are asleep—and you are beautiful. I know it might seem wrong to call a boy beautiful, but you are not old enough to be handsome. The orange light plays with the features of your young face to reveal an inner peacefulness. As I watch you sleep your expression changes—from happy to sad to ferocious—with every flicker of the lamp. Shadows over a lip, light caressing a cheek, eyes darkened with contempt, chin aflame with pride.

I wonder how many wars began because of what fire betrayed. When it does this to a sleeping child, what did it do to Tecumseh or Sitting Bull? How many have been doomed by an ill-timed spark from a poorly placed log?

A man has only as many expressions as fire will allow. It is a strange thing, fire. I know, for example, that sometimes it has an effect that's opposite of what's intended. When it's meant to be warming, it's cold. When it's meant to offer friendship it can convey hate. When it should have been feared it was thought to be warm and inviting. In me, when my father intended the flame to crush me, it spawned strength and hope.

I watch you, my son, sleeping. You are exhausted

from the trip here and the day's events. Your lips pursed, mouth slightly open, I press my hand on your chest, as I have done a thousand times since you were born, just to be sure your heart is beating.

I'm not sure what I would do if I could not feel the rise and fall of your tiny chest. As I write this I choke back tears. God, how I love you, little man.

Sometimes I wonder how such a great gift can be such a joy and burden all at the same time. It's surely God's cruelest gift. You love something more than life itself knowing it may be taken from you at any time. You will do anything to protect it from the type of pain and suffering you have experienced in your life. There is nothing real parents wouldn't do to protect their children.

You never want them to experience pain or suffering, yet you expect them to survive the trials and tribulations you have, and to be stronger than you. You want this child to be healthy and happy without going through what you have. It's crazy, isn't it? When I write it down I know it's impossible. Only through hard work are calluses born; muscles are built by lifting heavy burdens. Why should the mind be any different? Difficult times must fortify the spirit, not crush it.

As parents we do unusual things to protect the ones we love. But is it ever enough? Have I killed you with kindness? If I water the prized plant too much do I drown the very thing that makes me so proud?

Have I fed the goldfish too much—so much that its stomach bursts?

The world is full of demanding, spoiled children. Full of mothers and fathers without the heart, the resolve, to punish them. Little Donna will learn to hate us and young Billy will throw a tantrum if we refuse them more candy. But who is accountable for the twelve-year-old who is thirty pounds overweight? Isn't that another kind of abuse?

Isn't there some civic obligation to protect the health and well-being of children? And what of moral obligations? How many make the time to take their children to a place of worship? It doesn't matter which faith, any will do. A place that teaches some sort of dedication to something; a place where a person can make peace with him- or herself. A place where a person can reconcile, understand the sins of their past. A place where a person can say, "I'm sorry, God. I'm sorry for what I have or haven't done." A place where one can ask for forgiveness—for being human.

That, my son, is what we are lacking: the ability to realize that we are, in fact, merely human. We are prone to make mistakes. Some make them over and over again. Is it lack of guidance? Intelligence? Or have we, with all of our great wisdom, simply begun to think of ourselves as gods?

With all the crime, decadence, waste, selfishness—choices, all—have we stumbled upon the realization that we control our destiny?

We alter our bodies to suit our vanity with drugs or surgery; we make life or death decisions to fit schedules, our "plan" for our lives.

Are we not playing God?

Did I not, tonight, myself act the part of a deity?

I write to you with bloodstained hands, instruments of a mind that chose, godlike, to end not one, but two lives. The question is, how far will I go?

In writing, I think I can forgive myself. Not every temple is a place of worship; not every place of worship, a temple. Sometimes a man finds peace and reconciliation in the most ungodly of places.

I pray you can do the same.

IF MY TORMENTORS EVER caught sight of the hope I'd discovered, they would have gone to any length to beat it out of me. The burn became a badge of honor. Alone in the fields, I displayed it proudly— to the crows, cows and other animals.

For the first few years of my life I was dumb, a common mule. I woke, ate what was shoveled at me, worked when told, sat and slept where and when allowed. I made no choice, looked forward to nothing. A mirror, I am sure, would have shown me the mule's blank stare: darkness, lifelessness, no hint of anticipation.

I had to be careful. The mule that resists too often is taken out back and shot. Yes, my son, this mark *was* hope. And each night I would run my fingers over it before succumbing to sleep because it was given to me at a time of awakening. No longer praying for death, I rejected the life of a captive. I could and would get out.

While around my father and grandfather, I behaved even more respectfully, more downtrodden. I was never late getting the fire started and even quicker with every "Yes, sir." I would not, under any circumstance, look either of them in the eyes. My reasoning was simple. They were dominant males.

Looking someone in the eye should be a sign of respect, but these men saw it as a challenge to their authority. In averting my gaze I was letting them know I was not their equal, nothing but a slave to a master, beaten, hopeless. . . . Or so I wanted them to believe.

Which takes me to the next evolution of my newly found resolve. As I've told you, even the slightest outward display of independence led to a beating. Clenched fists, a puffed-out chest, extended jaw, to them, were clear signs of defiance. I could not afford to have them sense my newborn self-awareness because I had a plan—one that would get me the hell out. Where to, I did not know, or care. As long as it was away.

I actually began sleeping. My mind, while still not completely my own, allowed me dreams instead of nightmares. Visions of blood-soaked men beating me with chains as they set me on fire were replaced with images of houses with running water, soft beds and golden toilets. One night I dreamed of taking the paper money—and buying shoes. Store-bought, with laces and everything. And a clean, button-up shirt. And new overalls. I dressed and found a full-length mirror. I was so pleased with how clean I looked. My hair was cut and combed; the buckles of the overalls shone. The shoes blazed so white you could barely look at them. And then, as I was admiring myself, the girl from the mill walked up from behind and placed her hand on my shoulder. For some reason I wasn't surprised—it was as though I was expecting her. Her eyes were as dark as I remembered, but her hair was even more blond and sun-kissed. She did not say a word, just smiled. It was so revealing—so pure, so honest, it must have melted her father's heart a million times. She was happy to see me. Full of confidence, full of promise.

Finally, even if it was just a dream, I smiled back at someone.

Son, I was becoming human.

I HAD A PLAN. It was not a great plan—it was in fact a very, very simple plan—but it was a plan of my own devising. And no, son, clearly, I am not a great person; your father is a simple man, just as, back then, I was a simple boy. I wasn't about to concoct a great, complicated course of action—I'm not a philosopher, visionary, or liberator. And because I'm no Plato, Einstein or Lincoln, my plan was as common as the boy I was.

It was barely rehearsed and completely untested. I'd have but one chance, and my plan had to work the first time. If my grandfather or father caught even the slightest hint, the consequences would have been fatal.

This was nothing like teenage rebellion. I was in no position to argue over a curfew; I was not borrowing Dad's Chevy, bringing it back a half an hour late with a scuffed fender. The gas tank of this vehicle could never be an eighth low; the odometer never a quarter mile over the distance I said I was going to drive. No, son, this car had to return in pristine, exact, condition. Otherwise . . . well, I would not be writing this today. I had to guard my plan with my life, for my life.

Because I *am* writing, the way the story ends has already been revealed. Unfortunately, *because* I am writing, there is more I must tell. Son, if you are to fully understand where I sit at this very moment you will need to know exactly how I got here—and where I am going.

But to be honest, sometimes I'm not quite sure. Maybe it is for you that I write—and maybe for myself. I suppose someday somebody will call it therapy. Better than psychoanalysis? I'm not sure, but damn, it feels good to finally tell someone—almost as if the wounds are beginning to disappear, the shattered bones mending, new skin replacing the scar tissue. Each and every cell of my body is responding, as if the bruises never were.

Night terrors will never again make me wake in a cold sweat, clutching pillow, blanket or whatever the hell else I can get my hands on. The death-pit images—me, hunting for the tiniest sliver of light—have faded. After tonight I will never again rise in a dark room, fumbling at the nightstand, praying that I find the lamp. There was a time, son, when these hands worked more like eyes. When, in the darkness, a block of wood, a stump, were markers, guideposts.

I've learned, son, God made precious few places devoid of some sort of light. Even in the deepest seas there are luminescent creatures. It's been put a thousand different ways. "The light at the end of the tunnel; you are a ray of sunshine." The Bible speaks of Jesus like this, too. *The way and the truth.*

Whether it's the crisscrossing spots of a movie premiere reaching far into a foggy night or the neon magnets of Broadway, we seek the light, mothlike. Human nature, maybe. We are born when we finally escape the darkness of our mother's womb, to move on our own, no longer physically connected to darkness.

That original dependence? The center of our universe, where we eat, sleep, breathe and live. It is incredible, isn't it? What gives us life is what we most desperately strive to escape. We cannot run fast enough to stake our own claim, to establish who we are.

How fragile we are, from conception to birth. Christ, we're vulnerable. But the chemistry, the biology or, hell, the machinery of it all means I can write what needs to be written.

I sit here at my grandpa's table—a table where I have never before taken a seat—and I wonder. I ponder all of these things, looking at you, looking at the lamp.

One is life, one is light. But which is which?

In you I see light, but I also see life. And in the light?

I can illuminate a room and not create life. But I can create life and not light up a room. A man can be in a perfectly lit room, but not alive. A man can live in a damp dark crawlspace and . . . still not be alive.

Life can be very cruel, son. And painful. What kind of God ties such great pain to such a great gift? I've spent a long time wondering how many forms pain can take. There are obvious, merely physical answers. Pain is stubbing your toe when you get up in the middle of the night. Pain is when you fall from your bike for the first time and skin your knee. Pain is when your twelve-year-old flesh is held against a glowing hot wood stove until the smell of the melting skin makes you pass out.

Is there a threshold, more physical pain than a person can endure? Sure. This perfect human machine was built with safety switches: other systems shut down when pain exceeds our tolerance, rendering us unconscious. That's why people with head injuries, terrible burns and severely broken limbs go into shock: protection of the entity. Protecting this thing that the system serves. If the entity experienced more, what would happen? Madness, surely.

And that's the other type of pain. The perplexing thing about psychological trauma is there's not quite the same mechanism in place to protect us, to shut the entity down.

People go mad every day: catatonic, mute, speechless. They may stare into a void for days, weeks, months and, yes, even years. So why do the safety valves kick in for some and not others? Are some just stronger?

Why is it that when one man is faced with a crisis he maintains, does not waver from his daily routine, while another man faced with the same circumstances takes to living on the street, collecting other people's trash, eating scraps or sermonizing to anyone with ears? I wonder: who is better off?

While the "stronger" man perseveres, every day he is consumed. It's *Moby Dick,* ever elusive, but ever present. The scar tissue builds. Not forever, mind you.

Eventually the scars of the mind scab up and heal over. It takes as long as it takes: however long our God has allotted for us to either forget or forgive and move on.

Is this the same God that creates men so evil that they will beat and humiliate their own flesh and blood? How does He allow it? Why does He? Is God so cruel, or wise, that he would in fact sacrifice his own Son for the greater good? And is this the same God who allows us to experience joy? The joy of seeing my child wake in the morning, voice raspy, hair tousled, unsteady on his feet.

He allows these same pain-carrying neurons to also carry the gentle touch of a mother, father or child. As you sleep, I touch your face, your neck and run my fingers through your curly hair. You don't wake, but you smile at the caress.

It is pain and loss, son, that allow us to fully appreciate this moment—comfort and love.

The same hand I am stroking your hair with has spanked you when you've misbehaved. One hand; different sensations. We choose what we do with these hands. We create life, or take it.

I am writing to you to better explain the choices I've made—that I'm going to make.

As much as I have tried to keep you from the horrors of my past, I can no longer.

Did I have a choice? Maybe. Maybe not.

You will learn, son, that sometimes your choice is no choice at all.

I DID MY BEST TO DO what was asked of me, but the beatings continued. My grandfather left for a few days every month or so and, as always, went directly to the old mill when he returned. An even more careful watch on me was kept in the days following a return, and I never again ventured near during that time. Cowardly? Yes. Self-preservation? Yes, too.

I was locked up early in the evening for a week after Grandpa returned. While I once dreaded being down there, I now welcomed the solitude. I had the opportunity to work on my plan. I began to crawl around, exploring my dirt-floored jail, and got to know the underside of this house as well as they knew the rooms above. I would make my way to the area below my father's room silently and wait for him to stumble to bed. Although it was dark I would put a picture together in my mind, a map of where everything was. I knew the exact spot where he threw his heavy boots each night, and the borders of the creaky bed into which he flung himself. The groan of its frame also meant that his snoring would begin momentarily.

I paid particular attention to my grandfather's movements—especially when he would lift the floor-boards to retrieve his treasure chest.

After some time I could make my way around the foundation beams quickly and inaudibly. I could get to their rooms as quickly as they could.

Every night I would practice, snaking my way through vegetables, rats and spiders trying to beat the old man to his room. I became very good at this game. I played at becoming one of the silent, running rats. The vermin that once terrified me now studied—and perhaps even accepted—me as I infiltrated their world. I began to think of myself as one of them and I think that they thought the same of me. Soon, they gave way to the largest of their kind. They gave way to me: the King of the Rats.

Offering them scraps of food made them trust me. I no longer tried to scare them off the vegetables, which, I suspect, was the main reason I was allowed my crawlspace bedroom at all. No longer setting the traps given to me by my father, I let the rats roam free in my world. And they let me roam free in theirs.

I stretched out under the floorboards of my grandfather's room for so many nights that I soon knew exactly where he kept the paper money. It, of course, was the key to the success of my plan. If I could get the paper money I could get the hell out—of hell.

Because the treasure chest rested between a set of floor joists and sat low enough so the floorboards could be replaced without giving any hint to what was hidden below to anyone searching from above, it also meant the box itself was relatively easy to find from below—and take apart.

Once I figured out how to do this I could remove the treasure chest. While I couldn't see anything, I could take inventory with my touch. I knew what each item was from the first viewing I had with my father, and buried in among hair ribbons, pendants and rings was the paper rolled tightly with a rubber band. There was a significant girth to it, about the diameter of my fist.

I was careful to replace the treasure chest's contents precisely after my explorations, because even though I knew I could get the treasure, I still had to figure out how and when I was going to leave.

It had to be at a time when there was enough paper money for me to get the food and clothes I needed, and at a time when my grandfather and father were preoccupied to the point that they either would not or could not chase after me immediately.

Their behaviors were predictable, but only to a point. Every six weeks Grandpa would leave with a load of vegetables and return with more paper money and another item for his strongbox—and then hole up for three or four days. Now I must confess I suspected terrible things were happening in that old mill—things I could not imagine then, nor do I want to now. What I did know was that regardless of what was going on I had to make my break while it was happening.

Typically, when Grandpa returned I was directed into the crawlspace as soon as my father heard the engine of that old truck coming down the road. I suspect my grandfather drove especially slow to give him the time to lock me away.

I was left with enough water, bread and sometimes cheese for two days—though the lockup might last as long as five. A rusty pail served as my toilet, and I still had to chase my friends the rats away from it.

I kept careful watch on the inventory of the vegetables in the cellar, waiting and hoping for the piles to grow to the point where Grandpa would have to leave. If he put off the trip, the stench of decomposing vegetables would waft through the floorboards until it was so bad that even the old man couldn't tolerate it.

The next part of my escape plan was necessarily more complicated. Once I accessed and emptied the strongbox, then what? There could be no unsuccessful prison break—I would not get thirty days in the hole since I was already in the hole. . . . The only other punishment left was death, and I was not prepared to submit to that now. I had longed for it, once, as I lay with my face weeping pus and covered with dirt. I would lie for hours on end, face burning, legs, ribs, back all aching from any number of beatings, wishing I was dead. There were times, I am ashamed to say, I asked the rats to kill me. I would cover myself in vegetables, hoping they would see me as more of a meal. Jesus, can you imagine how desperate I had become? I wanted the rats to eat me alive.

But my desperation ended the night my father told me about the "others." About cities, clothes and indoor toilets.

From then on I wanted to live. To be alive. To experience things I couldn't even comprehend. I had to see it all for myself—water that ran when you turned a knob instead of pumping a handle. I knew I had to persevere if I was going to get out. One slip-up and I would never piss in a gold toilet.

Once I had the location of grandfather's box, I set my aim at finding a weakness in that prison. There were a few options. First and most obvious would be the trapdoor. It was located in the kitchen doorway, about five feet from the wood stove. Typical of trapdoors of its age, it was made of the same two-by-four planks as the floor. The only difference was that it had two strong hinges on one side and a flush mount clasp on the other. I wonder if the carpenter who constructed it ever thought someone would be trying to think of ways to dismantle it from the underside. Maybe—because there was no way to undo the latch from underneath, at least not without causing clearly visible damage to either the hinges or the latch. So, while the trapdoor was an option, it wasn't a likely one.

Then there was the set of double doors that led to

the crawlspace from outside. Their hinge assembly was similar to the trapdoor's. Heavy steel, each secured with three crude hex bolts. I spent a great deal of time in my nest at night, thinking of ways to defeat either the locks or hinges. I really couldn't come up with a reasonable solution that would afford me the secrecy I needed to perform either of these tasks. I knew that even if I could get a run at the doors, my scrawny body didn't carry enough weight to bust through, nor did I have the time or energy to pick away at the aged lumber.

So why didn't I just wander off while I was out tending to my crops? Well, that's a fair question. But the reality was, the pair of them watched me closely because, I am sure, they figured I would have to try to escape. Likely, they were both surprised and disappointed I hadn't yet tried: surprised because they couldn't understand how I could tolerate so much torture; disappointed because I wouldn't give them yet another opportunity to pound me physically and emotionally farther into the dirt.

No, simply making my way out of the cabbage patch wasn't a real option. My father made regular patrols, much like a prison guard, while his father, the warden, ran everything from around the house or the old mill.

"Don't be picken those 'uns there. They need to ripen up some, ya stupid sonofabitch. I swear you are as dumb as a sack a hammers."

He'd say these things and stand with his back to the sun, silhouetting himself, blinding me. I never saw the foot that kicked me in the chest or the powerful hand that would slam against my head. One minute I was being berated and the next I was lying in the dust, spitting blood. As much as a punch in the mouth hurt, this pain would go away after a day or two, but a kick to the ribs would stay with me for weeks. I remembered the kick with every breath I took— I only noticed a fat lip when I smiled or tried to eat. I didn't do much of either growing up.

My father's fighting technique was typical of most of the brawlers and bullies I have encountered. He'd always start with insults, tearing me down emotionally before he ever laid a hand on me. If I didn't resist he'd keep it up, calling me names, telling me I was a worthless, stupid, weak piece of shit. This could go on for seconds or minutes—until I either showed some defiance or he perceived defiance in my stance, eyes or expression. Then it really began.

"What?"

Slap across the face. Not hard enough to knock me down. Just enough to shame me, to make me look down, deeper into the dirt.

Walking around me now, eyeing me up and down: "You got somethin' to say, boy? You think you getting to be the man 'round here?"

Slap to the back of the head. Just enough to send

me forward a step or two.

Stopping in front of me, blurry because my eyes are full of tears of shame, hurt and rage. Tears burning my face like acid because I never want to give him the satisfaction of thinking he had actually hurt me.

"I said, you think you a man, boy?" Yelling now, closer, still blurry, like he's underwater.

Trying not to speak, I nod no. If I speak I can't prevent the lump in my throat from spilling open, loosening the floodgate on the tears.

"Can't you talk, dummy?" Push to the chest.

"You too stupid? When I talk to you, you better answer, cause I don't want no dummies 'round here." He knows that if I begin to speak I am going to start crying, that he's won again.

Push to the chest. Louder, blurrier: "You the man now?"

My voice comes as a whisper, desperately trying to contain the lump: "No, sir."

I'm not sure what he enjoyed more, watching me bleed after the beatings or watching me trying to maintain an ounce of dignity.

"Talk like a man, fer christsakes, not some skinny little sally girl." The stench of his tobacco-stained teeth and mouth makes me want to puke. Holding in long, deep breaths, I want to turn away, but can't. I try to look into his eyes to answer.

"No, sir," a little louder. My eyes glaze over. Cheeks

burning, hands clenched into fists, face distorting with the effort of trying to swallow that damn lump.

Open palm, heel of the hand striking my trembling jaw, teeth clamping on the inside of my cheek, blood filling my mouth. Eyes still underwater.

"Jesus Christ, you sure you ain't a girl? Fuckin' pansy. You better start talking like a man or I swear to the ever-living Jesus himself I will cut off your head and bury you where you stand." Louder, nose to nose: "Are you the man?"

"No, sir."

And then the lump is out. Tears flowing freely down my face, nose blowing bubbles, gasping for air, I don't even see the first punch or kick that sends me to the ground.

Stage two of the beating begins here. After the humiliation, the distraction, the takedown.

And then it's always the same—kick the ever-loving shit out of me. Several well-placed boots and I am rolling in the dirt in agony, hugging myself, hoping my sticklike arms can absorb some of the punishment.

"You sure you ain't no man now, are you?"

At the top of my deflated lungs I say it so loud and clearly it hurts: "No, sir, I ain't no man."

Sucking dust and sand into my bloody mouth, I can barely open my eyes. He looks over me in disgust, lights a cigarette and spits on me before he walks away.

This, my son, is the way it was. It would never be like the movies: your father, running through a field to imaginary freedom while soundtrack escape music swells in the background. The only soundtrack for me would have been a shotgun blast—slugs whizzing past my head, if I was lucky enough to hear them.

My escape had to go undetected for hours, ideally days.

The storm doors seemed more and more likely. My guardians would be less likely to notice tampering there because they were rarely used, and they faced away from the mill. In a perfect world, for them, they would have—but fortunately they weren't consulted when my makeshift jail was built. My ancestors had designed their cold storage only to hold the type of vegetable that does not plan on leaving on its own two feet.

SUMMER TURNED INTO FALL, inevitably. The crawlspace was almost filled to capacity with vegetables with what I'd harvested, and one thing that could not be seen: hope.

Fall is a funny time of year, my little man. The air goes from warm and comforting to damp, foreboding. And that's it. Trees, overnight, seem to lose their summer beauty and become ugly, black skeletons, waiting to grab a hold of you. I'm sure that's why Halloween is in the fall. There's no more miserable, frightening season. The trees creak and groan as the wind rushes, stirring fallen leaves, becoming deafening, terrifying you, giving the illusion that someone is always around, coming at you from somewhere, everywhere.

I wondered if this time of year could also be an ally. Could I become that someone in the wind, running anywhere and everywhere? I believed that the season could actually become camouflage and abet my escape.

Though I did not completely trust it, I knew I would have to form an alliance with the defender of the harvest moon. Fleeing any other time made little sense. I would never survive the winter cold. Tracks in the snow would lead them right to me. Spring's rain raised the same specter. In summer, while I was tending the crops, I'd be missed much too quickly.

I determined I'd have to try just after the crops were harvested, around the first frost. Hard, nearly frozen ground meant they would have a tough time tracking me.

The other key to success would be whatever or whoever captivated them down at the mill.

I will never forgive myself for making this part of my escape and I know I will suffer for eternity for my cowardice, but the fate of whoever was in the pickup when it returned to the farm was sealed. Mine was not. Am I reconciling, tonight? Only God can judge the decisions I have made; only He can wash the blood from my hands.

And worse, son, while it was not a certainty that he would return with a victim—I hoped that he would. Finally opening up and releasing these secrets. . . . More therapy? Confession is more likely.

It took me time to put all this together. I was getting stronger by late summer, and began to notice the old man eying me up, a little too closely. If I was too strong, too healthy, a beating would always come. If it was severe enough this time, my fall escape would become impossible. The tension in the house escalated. Was it the heat, poor crops, lack of rain or, I shudder to think, the lack of a playmate in the mill?

Whatever it was, they began to natter—not just at me, but also at each other. I knew from experience that once this started one of us—me—was going to end up lying in a pool of his own blood.

Regardless of the problem, I was always the cause.

Not enough rain; beat the boy.

Grubs in the cabbage; beat the boy.

Lightning took down a tree; beat the boy.

If the impending beating (and it was surely coming) came too early, I would inevitably get another just before my escape opened. If it came too late, I might not recover enough to flee. And so I had to plan my own suffering. It wasn't just about the timing, but the severity as well. Too light? I may get another for no reason other than to show me what a real beating was like. Too harsh and I may not survive.

With adolescence, I suspect, I was growing stronger, not just physically, but mentally as well. I prepared for the lashing with all the precision of a mission control engineer at NASA. There could be no clouds forecast on the day of my launch; no rain delays or dates for me.

My developing mind began to analyze and explore options. I calculated from my past just how much inventory the old man needed prior to scheduling a trip. I also calculated the length of time his libido would hold until he was ready to boil over, anticipating a new plaything for the mill.

When I believed the time was right I began to act out. It wasn't total defiance, just simple incompetence. I'd completed a chart in my head of my most recent beatings and the injuries I sustained:

- Unlit fire: broken ribs
- Burned dinner: broken nose
- Broken dish: black eye, maybe eyes, broken nose; not likely ribs or legs

And not only did I need to manipulate the timing, and the severity of the assault, I also had to make them think it took place on their terms, not mine.

Every day in every city in America people spend hour after hour learning how to manipulate others in order to get what they want, whether it's to win a contract, a court battle or an argument with a spouse. I suppose you could say it's my natural calling. Others manipulate to try to improve their lives. I was doing it to *stay* alive. Or, more accurately, to *become* alive.

I'm not sure that I could have done it as well in the business world. I can't imagine being in some meeting, nodding while some leather-faced, golf-addicted, martini-swilling hypocrite expounded on corporate policy, the stock market or whatever the hell else he felt he was an expert on. But I guess this is something each of us must come to terms with. People, on the whole, are hypocrites. They very rarely say what they mean or mean what they say. I'll give my father and grandfather one thing: they weren't hypocrites. If they said "it" was coming, "it" was coming—and watch out when "it" finally arrived.

Preachers can stand at pulpit and speak about virtue and how we must model ourselves after men of the cloth. These followers of Jesus . . . goddamned hypocrites. Minutes after a mass they're fondling an altar boy or choir girl. But what about you and me, virtue's victims? What of that young girl I saw being led into the mill? Where is she?

In heaven, with full halo and wings, playing the harp? Walking some restless purgatory, covered in blood, with my grandfather's skin still blackening her broken fingernails?

Or is she simply dead?

Son, we may find out soon, or we may never know.

When that first shovel breaks the ground, her blanket for all of these years, will her liberators stare at those empty eye sockets and understand what a beauty she once was? Likely not.

When she finally is discovered, and she will be, she will be work for someone. A small piece in the macabre jigsaw puzzle that that will reconstruct the events of today, yesterday and, hell, the past thirty-five years.

It is all just a jigsaw puzzle, my little man. But you'll never know what the picture is until that last piece is finally placed.

THE DAYS GREW SHORTER and the nights cooler. The crawlspace had just about reached capacity. With each piece of fruit and every vegetable I stacked time was running out. My dungeon was beginning to shrink around me; even the air became scarcer—at least that's how it seemed as I lay there at night, panicked.

It was as though I was drowning in a sea of vegetables. The acid of the tomatoes, the silky sweetness of the corn, the must of the potatoes—not only were they mocking me, telling me my opportunity would soon pass, but they made getting around the crawlspace all but impossible. It was something I hadn't anticipated, and I was close to the point of giving up. I still had no clear way of getting out, and strangely had not yet received a beating. I needed both. Immediately.

Son, there are those who do not believe in fate—and I am not sure I'm not one of them—but just as I was about to submit to those bastards for one more year, something happened that changed everything.

My grandfather was readying his truck for a trip to town, repairing something under one of the wheels, when somehow the truck slipped off the jack. The weight of the rear quarter panel wasn't enough to kill him, but it was heavy and painful enough that he had to call my father—who in turn had to call for my help. His tone of voice ensured that I ran immediately. When I got to them I saw my grandpa's legs trapped under the truck. The old man was writing in pain. I was breathless—only partly from the run.

"Git yer ass to that mill, boy, and grab that big ol' beam jack."

"Beam jack, sir?" I couldn't take my eyes off my grandpa.

"Yeah, you stupid sonofabitch. The one we used last year to prop up the house."

I knew what he wanted; I just wasn't ready to leave the scene. Seeing my grandfather in such obvious pain may very well have the most enjoyable moment of my short life. My father's glare, however, compelled me towards the mill.

I had seen the place many times from the outside, but never before crossed the threshold. That, I believed, meant certain death. Naturally, I suppose, terrified, I paused at the door. Would there be others inside? What would I say? Would they hate me because of who I was? Because of who they were? Would they think that I knew what was going on? That I had the power to stop it? That I even cared? All of these thoughts raced through my mind as I stood at the threshold. I suppose I was both disappointed and relieved when the heavy wooden door gave way: there was nothing inside the open room, only silence.

It was as dark and filthy as I imagined, a dirt floor covered in sawdust. Large timber columns supported larger timber beams, which in turn supported more timber supporting trusses, themselves supporting a wood plank roof.

The wind rushed in with me, stirring up dust and ghosts as I entered. I could feel them around me. The dust particles danced in the slats of light created by the ill-fitting boards. It was as though the light was magnetic, as though the only place in the room that the dust could exist was in the light. It was suspended, held in place, until finally it became exhausted and fell to its proper place on the dirt floor. I

I scanned the room, looking for the beam jack. I

couldn't find it and had to enter deeper. My feet made no sound, but in my mind it was like I was walking on sunburned grass. With each step I heard a crash, my feet burning, repulsed, eyes not wanting to see, skin desperate not to feel. I moved forward a few feet and saw the beam jack leaning against a column in the center of the room. Then I noticed, just above the jack, a chain attached to a pair of metal cuffs. The cuffs hung just about as high off the ground as I could reach. If my hands were inside those iron rings my feet would barely touch the ground. I froze and studied the column. It and the ground below were stained a horrible brownish red. Long strands of hair sat at the base of the column. It was then that I first realized: I had merely been beaten and tormented; I had never been tortured. I wanted to turn and run—run and never stop. I wasn't sure I had the strength to carry the heavy jack back to my father. My knees were weak and I wanted more than anything to vomit. And then I spotted it.

The brown, flowery printed rag was sitting on the workbench. I walked over to confirm what I already knew.

The dress of the only other human I had ever seen had been discarded, much like you or I would throw away an old paint rag. I picked it up. It was soft, and as pretty as I had dreamed so many times. I wanted to take it with me, to keep me comfort in the dark. If I had it with me, I fantasized, I would never be cold again.

And then my enraged father's voice intruded: "Get yer ass up here with that fuckin' jack."

I put the cloth back with much more care than when it was first discarded—right next to what I realized was my way out. I had seen my grandpa work on his truck enough to know that I was staring at an adjustable wrench. With this simple tool I could loosen the bolts on the crawlspace door hinges and gain my freedom. Without any thought at all I pocketed the wrench, grabbed the beam jack and never looked back.

I'm not sure who was yelling louder, my old man at me or his old man at him. I honestly didn't care. We set the jack under the back bumper and began to lift the truck off my grandfather's legs. When it was high enough for the old man to crawl out, it was pretty clear that his right leg was badly busted up. There was some blood, and the limb was bent at an awkward angle between the knee and the ankle.

"Jesus, Pa, we gotta get you to a doctor."

"Ain't no sonofabitch sawbones gonna get their paws on me." He tried to stand and fell back in agony.

"Pa, you can't even get up. Lookit yer leg, fer christsakes. It's all sideways."

"Shut yer goddamned mouth and help me up."

My father went to his aid—I wasn't being asked. Actually, it was as though I wasn't even there. My grandfather leaned on my father hard and tried to kneel. He collapsed again.

"Fuck me. Jesus fucking Christ."

"Paw, let me put the wheel back on, lock up the boy and get you to a doctor. In fact, it won't take me and the boy more'n an hour to load the truck up and we kin drop off a load a vegetables while we're in town."

The old man ran his fingers through his greasy, thinning hair, looked at me, then said, "Go get me a jug. It's gonna be a long fuckin' night."

Sweeter words I'd never heard.

I loaded vegetables with speed never seen before. They likely thought it was because I had some genuine concern for my grandfather. And that was fine; I wasn't about to tell them any different. About an hour later I was locked in the crawlspace with two days' worth of food and water, my urine pot and something they didn't give me—a key.

I waited for maybe five minutes after the sound of the truck had faded, but it seemed like an eternity before I made my way to the storm doors. It was pitch black, but I have yet to feel more light. I found the hinge bolts immediately and began my task quickly. When you're blind half of your life, your hands make excellent eyes when called upon. It took some convincing to get the bolts moving out of the old, hard wood, but bit by bit they loosened. With each crank I was gaining my freedom. It took all of my strength to loosen some of them, but I would have chewed them off if I had to. Like tumblers in a lock they fell to my crude key, the top hinge first, then the bottom. I was tempted, after freeing the top, to try to push my way out. But I knew I couldn't afford being injured, so I patiently worked on the bottom hinge as well.

Once the bottom hinge came free I was able to scrape my way out. I froze again, looking around me, at this place, at where I had just come from and took the first breath of my life. Deep. Satisfying. Mine.

I wanted to run, as fast as I could, through the forest and to the city, but I remembered my father's lesson—about paper money and how I would need it in order to get new clothes, food and possibly a place to stay. As the sun died in the west I did the most difficult thing I had ever done: I crawled back into that nightmare. I had to; I needed the paper money. Perhaps I shouldn't have emerged without it in the first place, but I had to experience the fresh air, the sun and the sounds, everything that a normal man takes for granted when he leaves for work in the morning. If someone needs to be reminded just how precious these things are, lock them up for a month, a week . . . hell, even a day. I guarantee they'll never breathe another breath without understanding what, at any given moment, can be taken away.

As I reentered my cell I had to recall the beatings, humiliation, starvation and pain to give me the courage to continue. I took deep, calming breaths, so I could do what I had practiced so many times. It was surprisingly easy. I likely spent more time convincing myself to get the box and the money than I spent on the actual act.

Son, too often we waste time fighting against what we know we must do. It is a lesson I have carried with me my entire life.

Climbing out the first time felt amazing, but leaving the second time was even better. The sun was setting, its orange glow reaching through the trees and touching my skin. I should have run like hell and never looked back, but for some reason I still couldn't. Beyond the house there was still the mill. Even though I really couldn't imagine what went on in there, I knew it was the place where the most evil of evil acts took place. And in the setting sun, covered in the shadows of its own eaves and dark rotted wood, it seemed to have an evil life of its own, as though the building itself was just as much a player in the horror as the living participants.

Strangely, I was drawn to it; I had to return.

My father and grandfather were long gone, but I was still scared out of my mind. Was it the way the sun's last rays were crawling over the wooden roof of the mill, long claws trying to hold on for just one more day, or was it the darkness inside the gray building, the weight of the events of so many years? Buildings and places do take on human characteristics. A bakery is a happy place to some, simply because of the smell. The baker could be the meanest man in town, but all of the children love the cakes and pies. . . . A hospital or old age home, full of caring people, makes many of us cringe with just its antiseptic smell.

The second time I entered the mill was different. The mystique was gone, but the horror was not.

I went straight to the workbench and picked up the sundress. Just having it with me I felt stronger, more sure than ever that I was going to successfully escape and never return. As I was about to leave I noticed a red can sitting by the door. I had seen grandpa pour liquid from it onto brush the previous fall, then set it on fire. I knew fire. And I knew that when you pour this liquid on it, fire really takes off. I found a pack of matches on the bench and did what instinct told me to do. I poured the contents of the can all over the mill, much of it on the center column. I made a trail to the door—just like Grandpa did when lighting brush—dropped the match, and watched the place come to life with light. I am pretty sure that that when I saw the flames take, licking the workbench, the column and the walls, I smiled.

Flames lapped up the sawdust and the evil of the place.

I'd finally made a good fire.

THE FIRE CAME FAST and hot. The heat jolted me into action. If it hadn't, I might have watched the whole damn place burn to the ground—and then set fire to the house.

As the orange glow engulfing the mill replaced that of the dying sun, there was no one to chase me, but I ran like there was. I felt great. My lungs were full of fresh air and my mind was full of new thoughts. Of other girls in sundresses, smiling, eyes full of life, inviting. No more despair, no more sadness: just joy.

The ground was cold under my bare feet but I didn't notice for quite some time. I made my way through the fields and into the skeleton forest. I suppose a normal child of my age would have been terrified. Not me.

I had no idea how long my journey would be, or where I was going. But the evil I was running from kept me going most of the night. I never felt the thorny brush that cut my legs, arms and face as I made my escape. And I was oblivious to anything that might have seen me as a midnight snack—animal, ghost, goblin or otherwise. In retrospect, you'd pity anyone or anything that got in my way. I was possessed. The only thing that could, and eventually did, stop me was physical exhaustion.

When I finally stopped, my lungs were screaming and my legs spent. I slowed to a walk and then, ultimately, a crawl. Fighting my body's every message, my mind kept me moving forward, crawling along the damp forest floor until, finally, my body did what it had to do. When it shut me down I simply passed out.

SON, IF I WAS WRITING a novel instead of a letter, this is where a chapter called "My New Life" would begin. But that too might be revised, simplified further. "Life," it could be rightly called—because prior to this point, I'd had none.

I merely *was*, existed because I was allowed to exist.

Prior to my escape I had no more purpose than a robotic welder. Outside of my duties I never did anything but be. Dig, plant, water and weed. Day in and day out. Dig, plant, water and weed.

It all changed the day I woke up in the forest. Actually, it was when I was *awakened* in the forest. The sun was in the midday sky, warm against my skin. The forest floor was still not completely dry, but the morning dew was disappearing. I know I was facedown because when I opened my eyes the earth I was sleeping on surprised me. Instantly reminded of where I was and what was going on—my simple plan was being executed to the fullest. I rolled onto my side and looked around me, staring at every rock and clump of dirt as only a person with new vision can.

I felt the toll that running a marathon inflicts: my thighs ached, my calves throbbed and my feet were bloodied and bruised.

And son, I never felt better.

I was alive and awake—not because of a verbal assault, but because my body told me it had had enough rest. Truly awake, I realized, I had some control—over me. I rolled onto my back and noticed how the sun streamed through the half-naked trees. Reluctant leaves—yellow, orange and red—still clung to the branches, knowing that once they lost their grip they would fall to the forest floor and, in time, become food for their parents.

There was no breeze to push them from their perch so they just hung, silent. I lay in silence, only the sound of my own breath confirming that I had not gone deaf. I was merely alone. Alone, with my life. My life. . . . Odd, that at that time, in that place, scarred and mud-covered, I understood that I had a life.

Every vein on every leaf, every needle on every pine, each curve of each bare branch was new to me. It really was like I'd regained my sight after years of blindness. Each rock and blade of grass that stood has been etched in my mind ever since. I breathed deeply and luxuriated in every particle of air that entered my new lungs. All the old pain was gone—the broken bones, cracked ribs and charred flesh, all gone. My body was new, healed: it was mine.

I got up on one knee, so full of questions and ready for any answer, wanting to take everything in all at once, wanting to inhale it all in one gulp. I don't want to say that I was giddy or drunk with what was happening, because that would cheapen what I felt. But I did want to drink it all in. Imagine someone long stranded in the desert being submerged in a cool, freshwater lake. You could drown in all of the new sensations, become engorged with everything you had been deprived of. Me? I'd been deprived of life.

Everywhere I looked, even in the dying of fall, I saw life. A squirrel scrounging for a long cold winter, a tree trying to shed its leaves so that an early ice storm would not cripple it. Thank God it wasn't summer—the abundance might have overloaded my simple brain. Finally, I stood. Shoulders back, chest out, arms by my side: I took another breath, and still felt human. I looked down and noticed myself. My feet were black with dirt and mud, my toenails long, rotted. My overalls were in tatters, bloodied, too, from running through the forest. I turned my hands front to back. These palms, callused well beyond their years, knuckles gnarled and swollen.

The body is a funny thing, my little man. A person can try to hide behind makeup and guile, but age always shows through. Still, those who have had an easy go of it seem to look younger than they are, while the rest of us seem older. Some of us, much older.

Character lines, they're often called. I have a different word: scars.

Look around any room and you can pretty much pick us out. We shouldn't be so damn old, but we are. People watchers try to fill the gaps. In bars, hotel lobbies and airports, they construct our stories—who we are and where we came from—from the lines on our faces. They wonder what the hump-backed old men looked like when they walked erect. They imagine what the painted, creviced faces of old ladies revealed in their youth. Beautiful? Just pretty? Neither?

Oh, the stories a body's scars can tell. Or at least begin. Only the soul wearing the body knows the whole story. Some of the most beautiful people in the world are burdened with the deepest scars; some of the ugliest, most beat-up, actually carry the least— inside, they may be the sweetest, happiest people in the world.

At that moment, I couldn't begin to imagine what someone would have thought of me—the story my pathetic state would tell. But I would soon find out.

I BEGAN TO WALK. There was no particular direction—I just walked. I can't say how far I went or how long it took, but eventually the forest began to thin. Soon, I could hear the rumbling of what sounded very much like my grandfather's truck. Instinctively, I crept towards the noise, while the barren trees did their best to hide me from possible detection. From one to the next I crept. Sure I was safe, I'd move on. I don't think I was afraid, just cautious. I didn't really believe that it could be *his* truck, but I couldn't be sure. As the noise grew louder I realized there was more than one truck. And they were both coming and going. Soon the trees thinned enough for me to see it: there were only two lanes, but the highway was marvel to me nonetheless. So were the trucks, cars and buses that passed. I hid in the ditch, mesmerized and, to be honest, terrified. I didn't think it was possible for anything to move that fast.

If the air the big trucks moved sent shivers through me, the small cars—of every color imaginable, with drivers of every shape and size—took my breath away. It was true: there were others, hundreds of them, flashing before me, speeding off into their lives, back to their homes to shit in their golden toilets. I wanted to leave with them, become one of them, but was too afraid to stand up and show myself. Any passing truck might be my grandfather's, and I wouldn't take that chance. Instead, I picked a direction and slunk along the tree line—following the road . . . to somewhere.

By following the traffic, I reasoned, I'd eventually get to a place where I could use the paper money for clothes, shoes and food. My body was speaking to me again, telling me it was time to eat. I had been hungry before but had no more control of when I would be fed than the family dog. Now I would eat because I wanted to, needed to eat. I would eat because I could.

As the sun once again began to sink in the western sky, my bare feet became numb to the cold and damp. I kept to the black road, heading towards what I dared hope was someplace warm and welcoming. The lights from the cars and trucks made sure that I didn't stray too far from this trail to my new life. And then, as I was cresting a hill, I saw the most spectacular thing.

Mountains of light reached into the evening sky. Hundreds, maybe thousands of them. They sparkled from the bottom of this hill, radiating through the valley like thousands upon thousands of diamonds. I had to double over to catch my breath before I could take one more step towards the shining city—down the gentle slope towards my future.

As the tree line disappeared it was replaced by large brick homes. There were cars parked everywhere. The large windows of these two-storey monsters were full of light and warmth. The smoke coming out of the tall brick chimneys wasn't acrid, dirty or angry; it was inviting, the smoke of alluring, happy fire. The dirt of the ditch gave way to a concrete path; tall metal posts, lights hanging from them like fruit, replaced my protective trees.

The unfamiliar surface made me nervous, as did the idea of exposing myself to anyone who might be looking out from those warm windows. But I had gone through too much to get to this point, to a place full of light, and nothing was going to stop me now.

There were many different roads, but the one I followed seemed to lead to the most light so I cautiously continued. Keeping to the shadows where I could, avoiding the exposing car and truck lights, I watched the large brick homes being replaced by buildings with much larger windows, more lights and flashing signs. Son, you know I couldn't read, couldn't possibly have known the buildings were stores. But I peered in the windows and saw amazing things. Large boxes with miniature humans moving in them, clothes—so many clothes—food and people. Lots and lots of people. They sat in one room, together, eating. There were long counters, men in white uniforms barking at women in pink dresses to pick up plates of food.

I felt for my paper money and wondered: if I gave them this, would they give me food, too? And then, I saw how these people were dressed—and noticed my own reflection in the window. Good lord, I looked half-dead.

My long hair caked with mud, my skeletal face scratched and bloodied; my sunken eyes yellow, my cheeks ashen. I scared the hell out of myself—I couldn't go in there.

A gap between the buildings offered plenty of darkness for me to hide my ugliness from the beautiful, clean, eating people. Could I ever be that clean and happy? I would never fit in with them; they'd run screaming, like I was some kind of a monster. I was so confused for a moment I may have even considered returning to the farm. Maybe I deserved no better. Maybe they were keeping me there because I was too ugly for the world of light. Maybe I *was* a monster.

My mind raced like this when a door opened and light exploded over me.

"Jesus Christ! Look at you . . ."

It was one of the white-uniformed men from behind the counter. He paused for a second, lit a cigarette and then noticed how uncomfortable the light was making me. Thankfully, he closed the door.

I could see the ember as he took a drag; it dropped to his side when he removed it from his mouth.

"What the hell happened to you, son?"

This is how the first conversation I ever had with someone other than my father or grandfather began. My every impulse told me to run again, but the food smelled so good, and I had so many questions.

"Happened to me, sir?"

"Yeah, kid, you look like you been through the wringer."

"The wringer, sir?"

He paused, perhaps wondering what he was dealing with. "Where you from, son?" he said, his tone gentler.

"I'm not sure, sir."

"You hungry?"

"Yes, sir, I am."

"Okay. Don't go anywhere. I'll be right back with a plate. I can't take you inside looking like that."

I did as he said and remained in the shadows, scared but exhilarated by the thought of food. A few minutes later light again filled the alley. Once more he kindly closed the door.

"Come here and eat."

I began to wolf down the meal. A hamburger and fries: it was the most delicious thing I had ever tasted.

"Whoa, slow down, son. You'll choke."

"Sorry, sir," I managed while shoveling in one fry after another.

"When was the last time you ate?"

"I'm not sure, sir." I could just make out what he looked like, and I'm sure he could kind of see me. He lit another cigarette and sized me up, no doubt trying to come to terms with who or what I was.

"What's your name, son?"

"Sir?"

"Yeah, what do they call you?"

"Stupid sonofabitch, mostly. Sometimes just boy."

"Boy?"

"Yes, sir, boy."

"Shit, that's not a name, that's what you are. You're

a boy." He looked at his feet and whispered to himself: "Nothing but a boy . . . *Boy* . . . Jesus. *Boy.*"

"You can call me Boy, sir . . . if you like."

"No. I don't like. No, I don't. A boy's gotta have a name." He took off his white cap, mopped his forehead and threw the cigarette to the ground. "How about we call you Tom? You like that for a name? Christ, you look like Tom Sawyer anyway, just a ragamuffin. Is that okay with you? Tom?"

"That's fine, sir. You can call me Tom if you like."

"Okay, Tom. My name is Henry. I own this place and I live upstairs. Can you tell me where you live?"

I hesitated. Would telling him mean I'd have to go back?

"You can tell me, Tom. Did you run away from home?" His voice was kind. "Did someone there hurt you?"

"Henry?"

"Yes, Tom?"

"I don't know where I came from—but I ain't going back. I did run away, I guess, and if you make me go back I'll just run again."

He drew a heavy breath, rubbed the back of his head with a chubby hand and said, "I won't ever make you go back. Jesus, Tom, if I did I'd be as guilty as the man who did this to you."

"Guilty, sir?"

"Don't worry about it, son," he said. There was a

quiet pause before he continued.

"Look, Tom, I can't take you to stay with me—and I am not sure that I want to take you to the cops. I think we need to get you cleaned up, get you some clothes and get you out of here. Have you spoken to anyone else since you got here?"

"No, sir."

"Good. Now listen to me, you just sit here nice and quiet. And don't let anyone see you. I'm closing up in a bit. I'll ask my friend Mary to take you in for the night. At least till we can figure out what to do with you." Sensing my fear, I guess, he put his hand on my shoulder and continued, "Tom, no one's gonna hurt you again. Not as long as you are around me, that is."

I'd never known affection; it felt good.

Even in the faintest of light, there was nothing there but compassion in his brown eyes. This wasn't a trick. I wasn't going to get a kick in the ribs for trusting him. This man was not my father. He left me to the darkness and I sat myself down on an old wooden crate until the light coming from the front of the building went out. Moments later I could hear Henry speaking with someone in a hushed tone. I could only imagine it was the friend he called Mary.

"Henry, I don't need this right now."

"You gotta do this, Mary. I mean, for christsakes, he's a mess. Just have a look. You know I can't take him. One room over a diner ain't no place for a boy.

You just gotta, Mary. It'll break your heart."

"Damn you, Henry. All right, let me see him."

The door opened, light again chasing away the darkness. And there stood Mary.

She was a stout woman, curly red hair framing a full round face. Her big brown eyes filled with tears the second she saw me. Henry stood beside her and I think there were tears in his eyes as well. He swallowed hard.

"Mary, this is Tom. Tom, this is Mary."

She moved closer, looked from my scraggly hair to my dirty feet and extended her hand. "It's nice to meet you, Tom."

I honestly didn't know what she was doing, and I tried to ignore her hand. Getting up from my crate I said it was nice to meet her.

"Tom, would you like to come to my house for a couple of nights? You could have a nice warm bath, get all cleaned up and sleep in my spare room." Her words were broken, but not forced. It wasn't like she was reluctant to have me, just that she could not believe what she was seeing.

I didn't know what to say. I really didn't. It had nothing to do with being overcome with emotion—I just didn't know what a spare room was and couldn't understand the concept of getting clean.

"Tom," she said, softly, intuiting my confusion. "Please let me take you home. . . . At least for one night. You can get some rest and maybe tomorrow we can talk about just how long you can stay."

She took me by the hand and for the second time I felt true affection. Our eyes locked then, just briefly. Hers pleading, mine questioning.

"It's okay, Tom. Really, it's okay. Let's go home."

Her hand was so soft, so warm, so caring and so safe—there was no way I could refuse. I knew I would be safe with Mary.

"Come on, my car's right over here." She pulled me down the alley towards an older four-door.

"Tom," Henry called after us. "I'll see you tomorrow and we can all talk then. Mary'll take real good care of you. Things will be a little clearer in the morning. I'll see you tomorrow, son."

"Yes, sir," I said.

"And Tom," Henry said, "I won't make you go back. Ever. I promise."

"Yes, sir. I won't go back. Ever."

I SUPPOSE, TO ANYONE else, the ride to Mary's house was uneventful. But son, it was unlike anything I'd ever experienced. From the roar of the engine, to the music coming from the radio, to the dash lights, to all the sights and sounds on the way: it was new. Things that most people take for granted, that would, in fact, be more shocking if they weren't there—cars, stores, lights, buildings, people. . . . Hell, even the traffic lights amazed me. I was a newborn in a ten- or twelve-year-old body: remember, son, I had no idea how old I was.

I remember making myself small in my seat as Mary asked. I guess she and Henry had decided that someone might be looking for me, hunting me down. I must have seemed so broken that even two complete strangers couldn't bear to give me up to my pursuers.

We didn't talk. She seemed focused on driving, while I focused on everything else. Bright store lights gave way to tall lighted posts again, and then trees appeared as we turned onto a darker street—one with much smaller houses than I had seen before. Some were dark.

"Now, Tom, you gotta be quiet when we pull into my driveway. We really don't want the neighbors to know you're here, okay, honey?"

"Yes, Mary, I won't say nothin'."

"That's good, Tom. Don't say nothin'."

The car turned onto a short road beside a small one-storey house. It was dark as we pulled up, almost to the back. A cedar hedge meant we were pretty well hidden.

Once she shut off the engine, Mary got out of the car and waited patiently. What she could not have known is that I had no idea how to open the door— I'd seen Pa and Grandpa use the outside handles to get into the truck, but I'd never been in it myself. Finally she walked to my door and let me out.

"Come on, Tom. Let's get you inside."

I followed her to the back door; she fumbled for a key in the dark. When she found the right one I walked into my first home.

Mary was careful, selecting lamps in the corners of rooms that would throw just enough light to let us see where we were going. She was smart that way, and kind. Somehow she just knew that I didn't want to be seen like this, revealed in the glare of a bright light. Or, maybe, it was because she really didn't want to see me in this state. I can't be sure.

"So, Tom would you like to have a shower and get cleaned up?"

"Shower?"

"Yes, Tom. You know what a shower is, don't you?"

"No, sir, I don't."

"Sir?"

"Yes, sir. Sir."

There was nothing at all contrived in what came next: it was quite possibly the most loving smile I will ever see. "Tom, I am a woman."

"Yes, sir, a woman."

Her hand covering her mouth, she tried not to laugh. "You don't call a woman *sir*, Tom. You can call a woman *ma'am* if you want."

"Ma'am?"

"Yes, Tom. Ma'am . . . Tom?"

"Yes, ma'am."

"Have you never seen a woman before?"

"No, ma'am." The word was becoming more comfortable to me.

"How is that possible? I mean how could you live your whole life and not see a woman? You must have a mother. Don't you?"

"Mother, ma'am?"

"You know, Tom, a mother and a father?"

"I got a father."

"No mother?" She looked at me, again, strangely. It wasn't her disbelief of earlier and it wasn't pity, but there was something about it that said, "Let me teach you something."

"Well, Tom, the mother is the woman version of a father. A lady father. The *ma'am* to the father's *sir*. Do you understand?"

"I think so, ma'am. And, no, I ain't got no mother."

"No, Tom, I'm pretty sure you ain't got no mother," she repeated and then looked away.

"Tom?"

"Yes, ma'am?"

"Well, Tom, you're in awful shape, you know that?"

"Yes, ma'am, I'm in awful shape."

"How did you get this way, Tom?"

"I don't know, ma'am. I just always been in awful

shape I guess."

"No, Tom, little boys like you aren't always in awful shape. Someone, something, has to do this to them. Who put you in this shape, Tom?"

"Ma'am?"

"Was it your father?"

I thought for a bit, then decided to trust her with the truth. "Yes, ma'am, it was my father."

MARY LED ME through the house towards a room.

"This is where you will be sleeping. Is it okay?"

My God, "the spare room" had a bed, a cupboard I later learned was a dresser, curtained windows and a warm carpet on the floor.

"Yes, ma'am, it sure is."

She smiled and asked me to follow her. When we got to the bathroom she turned on the light and showed me the sink, shower and the toilet.

"You know what a toilet is, don't you, Tom?"

"It's for shitting in, ma'am."

She smiled again.

"Ah, yes, Tom, but we don't say that. We say it is for going to the bathroom in."

"Ma'am?"

"Yes."

"Don't we shit in the toilet?"

"Well, yes, but please just say 'go to the bathroom.'

'Shitting' is just not a very nice word, okay, Tom?"

"Ma'am?" I had to ask. "Is this here toilet gold?"

She finally laughed—a real genuine laugh—the kind you couldn't contain if you tried, big white teeth dancing behind her soft lips.

"Why no, why would you ever think such a thing?"

I was embarrassed. Looking down at the fuzzy carpet I was standing on, staring at my black feet, I wanted to cry.

"It's all right, Tom." She knelt and put her arms around me and pulled me in close. She smelled like flowers. "I'm sorry. Please forgive me for laughing. I'm not so good with kids and I'm not sure I always know what to say."

I felt so good in her arms. So secure. I never wanted her to stop, but I also knew she felt bad and now I wanted to make *her* feel better.

"My father."

"Your father?"

"Yes. He told me that if we ran away to the city we could shit in a gold toilet just like Loretta Lynn."

She pushed back a little—not all the way—and stared deep into my eyes.

"Tom, there's no such thing as a gold toilet, but I can tell you this: Loretta Lynn shits, I mean, goes to the bathroom, in the exact same kind of toilet you are looking at right there."

"Thank you, ma'am."

"For what?"

"For telling me about toilets."

When she stood and started the shower, I was again amazed. Water came from the spout at the turn of a handle. And it was warm and clear.

That night I took my first shower. The water running around my feet as black as the dirt floor of the family mill—I was washing everything away. Cleansing. I was finally becoming clean.

Mary never actually left me alone, but she was also careful to respect my privacy. That really wasn't necessary because I knew no shame. She handed me soap and told me how to use it. The dirt reluctantly left my body, exposing scars and bruises I never even knew I had. After a while it seemed I could actually become as clean as those people I'd watched eating at Henry's.

Without looking at me she reached in and turned off the water. She handed me a large warm towel and told me to dry myself. I did as she said and wrapped the towel around me. Mary asked me to stay where I was while she went to get me something to sleep in.

"This is one of my old nightgowns, but it should be okay for you to sleep in." She handed it to me and turned again.

I looked at the pathetic pile of my old clothes and knew that I would never put them on again. What I didn't know was how to put on the nightgown.

"Ma'am?"

"Yes."

"Thank you for the nightgown."

"You're welcome."

"Ma'am?"

"Yes?"

"How does it work?"

Her dark eyes were dancing in the bathroom light as she rolled up the nightgown and put it over my head. She told me I could let go of the towel.

Son, I suppose you must be wondering why I am going into such detail. I guess it's because that what may seem like small events, to me, were life-changing. As I said earlier, I was like a newborn trapped in a boy's body. The kindnesses that Mary and Henry showed me helped shape who I am—and who you are—today. If I'd had the misfortune of running into less caring souls, I might not be writing you this letter. I feel it's important—for you to fully understand me, my mindset and the decisions I have made tonight. And to do that, you need to know, at least a little bit, about the people, places and events that made me.

Mary apologized that she had nothing more appropriate for a boy to sleep in. I told her it was warm, soft and smelled like spring. I couldn't have been happier or more comfortable.

When she looked at my old clothes, she said, "I'll

try to wash them, Tom, but I expect it'll be better to just go get you some new ones."

"I got paper money, ma'am, for new ones. My father told me I could get clothes and shoes with the paper money." I reached down and took out the roll from my pocket.

It was Mary's turn to be surprised. "Where in the world did you get that, Tom?"

"Will it get me clothes and shoes?"

"Yes, Tom. Yes, it will. But tell me, where did you get this?"

"I took it."

"Took it? From who?"

I hesitated, thinking I'd done something wrong, but felt safe enough to respond.

"From my grandfather. My father showed it to me one night and told me that if we took it we could buy clothes and shoes. So when I left, I took it." I handed her the roll. "Do you think you could get me some clothes and shoes with this?"

It's quite possible she'd never seen so much money at once. "Yes, Tom, lots of clothes . . . and lots of shoes."

She released the bills from the rubber band and inspected the pile carefully. "There has to be three thousand dollars here, did you know that?"

"Is that enough?"

"More than enough."

"I wanted the shiny money, but my father told me that it might be prettier than the paper money, but it ain't worth as much. Is that right?"

"Yes, that's right."

"I'm thankful he told me that."

"Yes, Tom, I'm sure you are. Tom?"

"Yes, ma'am?"

"Do you mind if I hold onto your money for you?"

Without hesitation I told her I did not. Then I asked her if she would take me to get some clothes and shoes. She said she would and we stood there quietly for a few minutes. Then she put her hand on my shoulder and asked if I was ready to go to bed. I told her I was and she led me back to the spare room. She rolled back the covers, fluffed the pillows and told me to climb in.

There's really no way to describe what that bed felt like. But think about when you lay down in a really good bed. Maybe it was in a hotel, or a rich friend's house—it felt just like that, multiplied by a thousand. My body sank while Mary covered me with the blankets. The top one, a heavy quilt, felt restricting and comforting at the same time. She told me to rest my head on the pillows. It was the one sensation I didn't like. She must have sensed it and asked me if I was okay. I told her I had never had a pillow, so she took them away. Just like that—no comment about me being ungrateful, stupid or anything. One minute they were there, the next, they were gone. And I was floating, like some sort of king, in a heaven-sent bed.

Mary looked at me the way a mother looks at a son. The way I look at you now as you sleep on that chair. She bent down and kissed me on the forehead.

"Good night, Tom."

I wasn't sure how to respond but followed her lead. "Good night, Mary," I said.

THE BEST SLEEP COMES when you're totally safe and completely exhausted. I was covered on both counts. I had never been so secure, had never known affection before that night. I'd never known a gentle touch; hands didn't caress, they punched you in the mouth. It's crazy for even me to think, as I write you, son, of a grown man punching a child in the mouth. But it does happen. Did happen. Every couple of weeks I read of a baby being shaken to death or starved, of a daughter murdered by a father. The same man who, just hours earlier, was pleading to the world on CNN for her safe return, knew she was lying, with a friend, cold and lifeless, in an unmarked grave in some goddamned field.

There have always been and always will be evil people, monsters preying on the easiest of targets: those who want nothing but their affection, their love. The more my father beat me, the more I wanted to please him. I was very much like a battered wife or, even more instinctually, the beaten dog that keeps coming back to an abusive master. I know how insane this sounds, but I clearly recall how much I wanted to make my father *happy.* Maybe the beatings would stop. Maybe if he were happy, if he didn't feel so bad, then he wouldn't beat me. Maybe the beatings were my fault. Maybe if I acted a little better. . . . Maybe.

Regardless, that night I felt safe. I could rest, sleep without fearing the ramifications of not waking in time to light a fire. I was exhausted, yes, but I didn't sleep because I was exhausted, I slept because someone had asked if I wanted to go to sleep. There is a difference between sleep that comes because you need it and the sleep that comes because you want it. The difference is waking when you want to wake, instead of when you're told to.

Closing my eyes, I thought not of my father or grandfather, but of Mary. Far away from the farm-house, the abuse, the pain and the torment, I'd like to say I dreamed, but I didn't. Nothing. That first night in a real bed in a real home I merely slept. Possibly, it was exhaustion, possibly just that I was in a real bed, aboveground, with the bathroom light conveniently left on to throw its warm glow over me. My eyes closed with warm thoughts and did not open again until the sunlight pried them apart the next morning.

I can't say I was confused, not really. I'd always needed to be alert, aware of things going on around me when I woke. The room was beginning to fill with the natural light of the day, not fully lit, but bright enough for me to make out where I was. I remembered the events of the past days. Feeling the weight of the quilt, I almost didn't want to move.

I suppose you could say I felt guilty about just lying there, warm and comfortable. There was no screaming for me to make breakfast; there were no rats scrambling for shadows to hide in; and my skin wasn't so incredibly itchy that I wanted to scratch myself raw. Lying there, I just was. And I didn't know what to do. When you've been told what to do for so long, then you're no longer told, it's like you're lost. A convict set free should be happy, right? But what do you do when there are no guards telling you what to do twenty-four hours a day?

As I tried to figure out what I was supposed to do, my nose told me. I was scared at first. The smell of bacon had become its own scar. But understanding, somehow, that everything here was different I got out of bed and followed the smell to the kitchen.

The flannel hem of the nightgown I still wore dragged behind me as I made my way.

I'm not quite sure if Mary had even slept, but I am sure there couldn't have been a more welcoming sight. She was standing at the stove taking as much care in turning the bacon as she had in tucking me in the night before. I don't think she noticed me because she went about her business, quietly humming. It was a song I'd never heard.

The sunlight was climbing the walls, gently, letting us get ready for it. Mary wore a blue housedress covered in white flowers. Around me, I finally took in the furniture of what I would now call a very modest home. A chrome dinette set nestled into the only full wall of the friendly kitchen. A strip of pink wallpapered flowers accented the sunny yellow walls. There were windows in one corner, each facing a different direction, and one above the sink. There was enough natural light coming through them that turning on the ancient fixture hanging above the dinette was unnecessary.

Moving from the carpeted hall into the kitchen even the transition from the cold peel-and-stick tile was warming. Mary floated, stirring, humming, smiling. I didn't want to disturb her. Someone that happy should never be disturbed. Even if the house caught fire I am not sure I would have said anything. Was I really as happy seeing her like this? As happy as she seemed? It's one of those moments that become forever etched in your mind, one that takes over all of your other senses. Tunnel vision. There is no bacon smell filling your nostrils, no cold tile floor under your bare feet; broken ribs don't scream for attention, hunger pains are silent and all fear is gone. All that remained was this vision: angelic, I guess. Yeah, I know how it sounds: Mary was an angel, sent from God to help me at just this moment. But in some ways I truly believe that from the moment she was born she was meant to be standing in front of that stove making bacon for me. And even if that was all she ever did in her life—and I'm here to tell you that's not true—she should be canonized. Saint Mary. I write it now because she would never let me say it. Mary, you are a saint. Thank you. Thank God for you.

She stirred a while longer, then picked up a piece of bacon between the tines of the fork and turned it carefully. And then she shook me out of my stupor by saying, calmly, quietly, "Good morning, Tom."

My new name didn't register immediately, and she turned to me, fork in hand, smiling. "You must be hungry, Tom. Sit down over there." She pointed to one of the chrome chairs. "I'll get you some breakfast. It's almost done."

"Thank you, ma'am."

"You found the bathroom all right?"

"Yes, ma'am."

She turned back to the bacon and checked the oven for something being kept warm. "Did you have a good sleep?"

"Yes, ma'am. I slept all night."

"That's great. I'm sure you needed the rest."

"Yes, ma'am, I'm sure I did."

While she hummed and cooked, I sat and waited. It was awkward for me—to just sit and wait. I was the one who did the cooking; others waited.

"Tom, how old are you?"

"Old, ma'am?"

She hesitated, like she was readjusting, remembering just what she was dealing with.

"What I mean is, your age. Do you know how many birthdays you've had?"

I desperately wanted not to be so stupid, but I had no idea what she was talking about. And I'm sure she realized this, because she jumped in before I could answer, trying to figure out a way to put it so I'd understand.

"Do you know what winter is, Tom?"

"Yes, ma'am."

"Okay, Tom, how many winters can you remember?"

I thought hard—I could count from the work I had to do on the farm, and I wanted to be as right as I could. I recalled everything that had happened, every spring, summer, fall and winter, all the beatings, non-beatings, good crops and bad crops. I figured I could remember maybe eight or nine years with confidence.

She did the math quietly and said, "I guess that makes you around eleven or twelve, depending on how good your memory is. And you know what, Tom, from the size of you that seems about right. Twelve it is."

"Twelve?"

"Yes, Tom, you are twelve years old."

I think she knew that I really couldn't grasp the concept, left it alone and announced that breakfast was ready. She opened the oven door and took out a few tin plates. They were full of eggs, toast and pancakes, and with the bacon she piled some of everything high on a glass plate in front of me. The steam was rising as I sat staring.

"It's okay, Tom, go ahead and eat. I'll be right over here."

Now, the boils from the last time I'd had hot bacon had healed, but the scars in my mind had not. Mary stood waiting, so I felt like I had to eat. I started with what was most familiar. The white toast was crispy and buttery. It was warm, not soggy and half-chewed. I almost felt human, eating something that hadn't already been in someone else's mouth.

Mary smiled, tousled my hair and went to get herself a plate. She sat down across from me and began to enjoy her hard work as well.

I did my best to copy her movements, using a fork for the eggs, a knife to cut the pancakes. And dipping them in maple syrup . . . It was such a simple, surprising joy. Maple syrup! I wanted more but was too shy. I would have licked that plate clean if she hadn't added more food. I ate until I couldn't eat anything else. When I was finally done my stomach was so bloated I felt sick.

Even that felt great.

MARY TOOK MY plate away and I thanked her for the food.

"I've washed your clothes and mended them as best I could. They won't last long, but they'll do until I can go to get you some new things."

"Thank you, ma'am."

"Tom, I . . ." She paused, eyes not on me but somewhere in the distance, searching. "I found something in your pocket. . . ."

I guess I knew what she was trying to ask, but I was just as lost for words. What could I say about the sundress? I mean, truthfully, how could I explain a girl I never knew, tortured and likely murdered by my father and grandfather? Would I be blamed for her death—like I'd been blamed for so many other things?

The truth might make Mary try to find them. And what then? What would they do to Mary? I thought of what I endured after catching just a glimpse of the girl. I couldn't risk them knowing anyone else knew, especially not this woman.

So I did what I thought was best: I lied to Mary.

"The dress, Tom—where did you get it?"

"I found it."

"Found it?"

"Yes, ma'am."

"Why did you keep it, Tom?"

"I guess I liked it. It's soft."

She looked at me with a skepticism I now understand this way: it was the look a parent gives to a child they want to believe. The look of someone who knows she is being lied to, but who doesn't have the courage to confront the liar. More parents need to know how to put that look into words. Who knows how many kids would be alive today if a parent had just said, "No, I don't believe you. I'll drive you home from the party." Son, too many times these are the last conversations parents never have with their child. If only. If only that questioning look became a real question.

Son, I looked at Mary and told her what I had to.

"I'd like to keep it—if I can."

Mary wanted to say something, but held back. Finally the words came: "I put it and your clothes back in your room while you were sleeping, Tom. They are on the dresser."

"Thank you, ma'am."

There was no "You're welcome" now. We sat silent for a moment, Mary unsatisfied, and me sick with guilt.

"Go get yourself dressed and I'll clean up this mess, Tom."

She forced a smile and I went to my room to find the clothes and sundress, just as she'd said, neatly folded on the dresser.

In my familiar clothes I sat on the bed and held the fabric. The scent of the girl who wore it washed away, down the same drain as the dirt from my clothes—from me. Why was it still so important to keep it close? And why did I still feel so dirty?

When I wandered back to the kitchen, Mary was still finishing up the dishes. She was no longer humming, just going about a job as though it was a job.

"I'm just about done here, Tom. Then we can talk a bit more," she said and sighed.

I felt even worse about the lie I'd told her—but not bad enough to offer the truth. When you're trying to survive, there's no telling what you're capable of, my son. When a man—a boy, in my case—is backed up against a wall, he makes rational decisions that seem completely irrational to someone not backed up against that very same wall. Sitting with your morning coffee, reading about some incredible event in the morning paper, it's too easy to say, "How could he?" But if you've never been backed into a corner before, never had to take a chance or risk a difficult decision that disrupts your comfortable life, how can you really know? I've learned that often the people quickest to judge have never faced this type of decision.

You'll hear it too, son: some men are born into greatness; others have greatness thrust upon them. In my case—our case—something very far from greatness was thrust upon us. Actually, when I think about it, the situation I was in, that I am in—that *we're* in now—is more of a "born into" kind of thing.

No one walked up to me and said, "You look like you'd handle torture really well, so why don't you go live with these two sadistic bastards. . . ." No, I won that lottery all on my own. One minute I wasn't; the next I was.

The same is true for you, my little man. You never asked for this—you just *are*. I guess I'm sorry—for bringing you into it. For having you? I'm not. You bring me more joy than you can imagine. God, I love you. And what about you? Well, the word *misery* barely covers what I bring to our relationship.

I know I'm not totally at fault, but I have made choices over the course of my life, and your life, and in fact tonight, that tie our fates. Good or bad, the die has been cast and we will both have to face this together.

From that first lie to everything that's transpired tonight, I will not apologize. Could I have done things differently? Certainly. But would the outcome change? Likely not.

Wisdom is something you only get in retrospect—

by living through certain things. Yes, sometimes a man can learn from the wisdom of others. But for me, for us, who was there to turn to? Who else had ever been in my shoes? No one I knew. Jesus, at that point in my life I'd spoken with only four people. And two of them I never wanted to face again.

Lying to one of the two I wanted to trust me was not a great way to start, but tell me, son, what other option did I have? If I told Mary the truth I might have lost her forever. Back against the wall, something primal took over. Not a great moment in my history. Did I hurt Mary? Likely. But would I have hurt Mary more by telling the truth? Maybe. And that I was not willing to risk.

God, Mary, I'm sorry. You were so open with me and I lied. But even after all these years, faced with the same situation, I'd do it all over again. Sometimes you have to lie to protect what you love most. And at that point, you were what I loved, Mary. . . .

But tonight is for confession. Tonight, my son, is for the truth.

THE DISHES WASHED and dried and put in their place, the dishrag and towel carefully folded and left on the sink to dry. Mary patted the front of her dress and turned to me. Something about her face changed: I think she had just resolved an internal debate—the heart of which was the sundress—and at precisely that moment put it to rest.

"Okay, Tom, we need to get you some clothes. How would you like that?"

"I would like that very much."

Finally, she smiled again—and began sizing me up. It wasn't like the night before, when she hardly could believe the state I was in, but it was a look of acceptance, a measuring from the distance created by the brown sundress.

"Well, this won't do," she murmured, and then left the room. Returning with a rolled-up piece of plastic, she immediately went to work running flexible tape down my arms, legs and feet. She was writing things down and whispering to herself as she did this. Of course I had no idea what she was doing, but I complied with her every command: to stand straight, move here, look there. I enjoyed the attention for some reason. But I guess that's not so hard to understand. I enjoyed the physical connection. And I was fascinated, watching her run this thing over my body, wrinkle her brow, write, stand back, pause and write some more. The whole exercise was pleasurable, entertaining. When Mary was working on something she was fun to watch. She was fun to be around—just to be with.

I suppose she had enough of measuring me, and I think I'd had enough of being measured, when she said, "Tom, I'm going to go get you some clothes.

Do you think you will be okay here alone until I get back?"

Okay? I'd been left with barely enough bread and water, in a crawlspace of a house, for days on end. "Yes, ma'am, I'll be okay. But ma'am?"

"Yes, Tom?"

I was reluctant to ask, because I had never done this before. "Do you think I could rest for a while . . . when you're gone?"

She looked concerned. "Of course, Tom. You poor thing, you must be worn out. Of course you can go back to bed."

It was such a strange moment for me. The sun was still shining and I hadn't done a single chore and she was telling me it was okay to go back to bed. Well, the truth is, I needed it. And Mary and I made my way back to the spare room where she pulled back the covers, got me underneath and tucked me in as carefully as she had the night before.

When I lay back and looked at her she smiled and told me to have sweet dreams and that she would be back before I knew it.

I floated there until I heard her leave, lock the door, start the car and drive off. And then I got out of the bed and retrieved the sundress. I got back under the covers and clutched that dress as though it was the most important thing in my life.

Some people do not remember their dreams, but

fortunately, and unfortunately, I do. I have to live, or more accurately, sleep with that.

At that particular moment I dreamed of great things and horrible things and, well, just things. But what I dreamed the most was the girl. The little girl, taken from her parents, her life and, oddly, me. I say she was taken from me because even though I never knew her, she was mine the moment I saw her.

The only remembrance I had was the dress I clutched while I dreamed of her cooking bacon on Mary's stove. Mary sat at the table with me and smiled as the girl turned the bacon. Just like Mary, she did it lovingly, as though each strip was as important as a child. Her large, dark eyes watched each spatter of grease jump from the pan to the counter, careful to remember so she'd know what to clean and make Mary happy. The girl smiled at me and at Mary then.

But quickly her smile changed to an expression of pain. The bacon began to spatter so ferociously she couldn't contain it. She was swatting at it with one of Mary's dish towels, but it was no use. Bacon grease hit her on the arm, her neck and then her face. She screamed as she tried her best to stop the attack. Mary and I could do nothing. We were paralyzed, glued to those chrome chairs as we watched the horror unfold. The girl I loved was melting right in front of us. Her skin was liquefying, like the wax of a candle. I was helpless, powerless. She became little more than a puddle on Mary's kitchen floor, nothing left but the sundress.

I was no stranger to nightmares, but this really shook me. I woke clutching the sundress even tighter and longed for Mary's return. I was sweating and warm, but shivered at the thought of the girl.

Son, I'm sure a psychologist would have a field day with this—and the rest of my life—but what's the point? If we're honest with ourselves everything else pretty much takes care of itself.

"Do you know why you're overweight, son?"

"I eat too much."

Truthful answer.

"Ma'am, do you know why you stole the car?"

"I wanted it."

"And you, sir, can you search your feelings and tell me why you killed your father and grandfather tonight?"

"Of course. I hated them."

So yes, son, I do have an idea of what that dream meant, but there's no need to go into it in this letter. That's one thing I'll leave between the grave and me.

I WAS STILL IN BED, somewhere between being awake and asleep, when Mary returned. She never had to worry about me after all: I never left the bed, except to get the dress. I was fully drawn back to the conscious world when I heard a car pull up to the house. I tucked the dress under the covers.

Mary came to check on me, and stood in the open doorway without making a sound. I could feel her presence and lay still, with my eyes closed, hoping she would come to me with a gentle touch. She lingered, but then quietly closed the door.

I resisted as long as I could, but the room was constricting and the thought of the new clothes forced me up. Making my way down the hallway again, I was anxious. I checked the kitchen first, but did not find Mary, so I began to wander the house. Now, I'd never had the freedom to roam like this, so every step into new territory was something of an event for me. To a lesser magnitude, I suppose, it was like man taking his first steps on the moon—each footfall new, exciting and somewhat terrifying. I wasn't sure if I should keep going, but like most explorers the need to know propelled me.

The house was not large. I did not have to venture far to find a very content Mary, seated on a plush lime green couch in a small cluttered room. She was sifting through bags of clothing, picking up items, turning them front to back and smiling to no one but herself. In her own world, I think she was imagining how the clothes would look on me. Any apprehension I had about the state of our relationship was gone.

As she inspected clothes, unnoticed, I inspected

the room. A large window overlooking the front lawn gave me my first daytime view of a neighborhood. From my vantage point I could see other small houses across the paved street. Almost every one seemed neat and tidy, with trimmed hedges and here and there the evidence of dying gardens. Cars, like Mary's, would slowly drive by, paying no attention to what was going on in any of the rooms in any of the houses. If any of the drivers knew enough to peer in this particular window they would have discovered true beauty: a woman, far past her childbearing years, carefully inspecting the clothes she was about to put on her newborn. It's a shame, really, because she wore such a proud, excited expression: she should have been seen. She knew she was doing something extraordinary, and it showed. If only someone else could have shared the moment. Still, son, I don't think anyone other than Mary would have appreciated the magnitude. How could they? And frankly, as excited as Mary was, I'm not sure even she could.

The window itself was framed by blue velvet drapes, which fell onto an equally blue carpet. The walls were a dingy off-white, but they did not for a second take away from the room's brightness. How much of the light was created by Mary and how much by the afternoon sun, I do not know. I do know I would put Mary up against the afternoon sun any day of the week. A number of leafy green plants were scattered about, and they too seemed to enjoy both Mary's and the sun's brightness. Actually, they were more than a little out of control.

Two worn wingback chairs were placed in corners of the room. The pattern of the fabric did not match the green of the sofa, but in my estimation that didn't matter at all to Mary. Next to one of the chairs was a small, wooden, book-covered table. A reading lamp stood behind it. The walls were decorated with pictures, forest scenes mostly: deer, majestic and free; ducks landing on a reed-filled marsh, with black dogs pointing to the unlucky ones that did not land of their own free will.

After a while I felt odd just standing, taking it all in, so I made a bit of a noise—nothing loud enough to startle her, just enough to let her know I was there.

"Oh, Tom, you're up."

"Yes, ma'am."

"Did you have a good rest? You were out for quite some time."

"Yes, ma'am, I did. Thank you."

"Well, I have some clothes for you here. Did you want to have a look?"

I sure did—but I just didn't know how to respond. This was the moment I had been looking forward to ever since I had hope burned into my flesh.

I began carefully: "If I could, ma'am."

"Come on over here then, Tom. I was able to get you some new shirts, pants, and look at these . . ."

She opened a brown box and held up a pair of white shoes—almost as white as the ones from my dreams. I stared, unable to speak.

"Try them on, Tom. Do you like them?"

"Yes, ma'am, I like them very much."

As it turned out, Mary was very good at measuring. She handed me an armload of clothes, placing what she called "briefs" on top.

"Now, these go on before your pants. They're also called underwear or shorts." Honestly, I wasn't sure what the thin, white material was for, but I did as I was told, carrying the clothes to the spare room. I closed the door and did my own inspection: there were a couple of pairs of briefs, short-sleeved shirts with no buttons or collar, long pants with no bib or suspenders, long-sleeved pullover shirts and some socks. If I knew what Christmas was, I would have thought that's what day it was. The clothes were soft and clean: I didn't feel worthy. Lord, who was I to wear such beautiful things?

I took off my old clothes for the last time and began to dress, starting with the underwear. Looking down my body at these new clothes, the feeling was better than my father ever could have described: it felt real; it felt pure. Purity was something my father could not express.

When I reappeared before Mary, she looked like a woman waiting to hear the results of a child's surgery.

Leaning forward on the green couch, hands on her knees, eyes wide and agonizing, she was dying for something to look at. Well . . . I was something to look at.

Her eyes became crescents and her hands rose to her cherubic face: thank God, neither my past nor my lie had ruined that smile.

"Oh, Tom, you look wonderful. . . ."

"Thank you, ma'am."

"No, don't thank me, Tom. It's my pleasure."

And I could tell that it was. There was nothing fake about Mary; she couldn't hide an emotion if she tried. Happy, sad, angry—you knew it; she was who she was.

"Turn around, Tom. Let me have a look at you."

I did as I was asked, not quite sure what was going on. She murmured, seemingly in approval.

"The pants may be a bit long, but I can hem them. The shirts look nice. How does the neck feel? Tom, is it too tight?"

"No, ma'am." I wouldn't have told her if I was choking, but it really was fine.

She stood, eyeing me from head to toe: smiling at times, frowning at others. Overall, she seemed satisfied with her choices. After I tried on a few more sets of clothes, Mary seemed more pleased and told me to wear what I felt comfortable in. I dressed in blue jeans and a T-shirt with some lettering on the front. She told me I looked good and asked me to come into the kitchen with her.

I immediately noticed a pair of scissors, a cape and what I learned later was a mirror, sitting on the table.

"Tom, would you mind if I cut your hair?"

Now, my grandpa insisted that my father cut my hair once in a while, so I knew what she meant. I just hoped it didn't involve the pulling, the tugging, the tearing his barbering meant.

I guess she could tell I was reluctant, and she reassured me: "Tom, it won't hurt. I just want to trim it a bit. You can stop me anytime you want."

Because I'd put all my trust in Mary, I told her she could. She sat me in one of the chrome chairs, covered me with the cape and set the oval mirror in front of me. Other than noticing my reflection in the pane of glass, I had never really looked at myself before.

I'm not sure what Mary saw when she looked at me, but I know what I did.

Thick, straw-colored hair hung almost to my shoulders. My ears were barely visible, just poking through at the sides. A thin neck supported my square-shaped head. My eyes were set back slightly, evenly spaced, and greenish-yellow—like my father's. They actually kind of scared me at first, because they were so similar to his. What other traits did I share with that monster?

Son, I think that's the moment I realized that no

matter how far away I ran, he would always be as close to me as the nearest mirror.

Once I got over that initial shock of similarity, I noticed the greatest difference: there, on my right cheek. It was burned into my flesh—the night my father gave me the strength to flee. The reddish scar was not hideous, not by any stretch of the imagination, but it was clearly visible. You could see the circles of the cast iron stove covers if you knew what to look for.

Mary stood quietly behind me as I took inventory of myself. It was as though she was waiting for me to discover the mark. What she couldn't have known was that it was the very reason I was sitting in her kitchen.

She leaned so I could see her face behind mine in the mirror, and began to touch my hair. She asked how short I wanted it cut; I told her it didn't matter, so she offered suggestions, using her fingers to show me different lengths. Whatever she thought best would be fine with me, I said.

She used a bottle of water with a spray nozzle to dampen my hair. Cut dry, I suppose it may have floated around the kitchen for weeks. A cut here, a snip there and she was quickly done. The whole event was completely painless—in fact, I actually found it pleasurable. I loved the way she touched me, so gentle. The hair stood up on the back of my neck when she cut it. There's always been something about having my neck touched. Son, you love it too.

There are nights when you can't sleep, and I let you lie on my lap or crawl into bed with me. If I'm not rubbing the smooth skin of your bare back, I'm playing with your hair. When I do this, you fall asleep almost instantly. I'm resisting the urge to do this right now. I have to be focused, finish this so we both can rest.

When my hair was mostly dry and set where Mary thought it should be parted, she asked, "What do you think, Tom? Do you like it?"

"Yes, ma'am," I said. "It's fine. Thank you."

In the small mirror I saw someone almost human and hoped that maybe I'd be able to fit in with the clean people I saw in the diner. What a difference a day makes. I watched myself smile, then automatically lifted my hand to the right side of my face and ran my fingers over my scar.

"Tom, I've been waiting to ask you . . . you don't have to answer if you don't want to, but I'd like to know."

I turned to her, still wearing the cape, feeling self-conscious about my self-exploratory trance. I couldn't see the scar now, but I could tell Mary was looking at it.

She drew me close and removed the cape. As she did, she held me in her arms—not long enough to make me uncomfortable, but long enough to let me know she cared. With her left hand she delicately touched my cheek, running her fingers running over each ring.

"Can you tell me about this, Tom? Can you tell me how it happened?" she asked. Her eyes welled. I know she couldn't comprehend this type of injury to a child; I also knew she knew I didn't do it to myself.

"I guess I can, ma'am."

"Did your father do this to you, Tom?"

"Yes, ma'am."

"But . . . how? I mean, what kind of a monster . . . to a beautiful little . . ."

Her words trailed as she turned away and put her hand to her mouth. She was trying to compose herself in the way so many women of her generation did. Her shoulders started to heave slightly and I knew she was fighting a lump in her throat, just like I had so many times myself. When the lump gets out, tears follow.

I did something then I didn't know I was capable of—I stood, extended a scrawny arm and put it on her shoulder.

"Ma'am, it's okay. It's okay."

"No . . . it's not okay. . . . None of this is . . ."

If I didn't really mean it, I may have started crying as well. But I raised my head and looked her straight in the eyes and said, "I am okay, ma'am. Everything is okay. Now."

I EXPLAINED AS BEST I could: how, in a fit of anger, my father held my face to a glowing hot stove as a reminder that I was always going to be his property. Mary made hot tea and she listened. She barely interrupted, letting me explain why I could never go back to the farm.

"Tom, we need to tell someone about this. This type of thing isn't done. It's against the law. . . ."

"Law, ma'am?"

"Yes, Tom. We have laws to protect people. We have policemen, authorities who are supposed to protect people like you. If we go to the law, they can lock your father away so he can never hurt you again."

"Ma'am?"

"Yes?"

"Will that mean they know where I am?"

"I guess, Tom, but you will be protected from them."

"I feel protected now. And they don't know where I am."

She looked like someone trying to figure out a riddle.

"But Tom, don't you want them to be punished for what they did to you?"

I thought a moment. "No, ma'am," I said. "Not for what they did to *me*."

Of course I had no idea what the justice system was or what it may or may not have done for me. I was just happy to be away. I was pretty sure that as long as Mary was by my side, no one would ever hurt me again.

"Are you sure, Tom? I mean, he did some pretty awful things to you. Terrible things. Things that a man should be punished for."

"Yes, ma'am, I'm sure. I won't go back. I don't want to see him again, ever."

She sipped her tea, then paused over my scar before saying, "Okay, Tom. I won't make you." Her brown eyes were strong and full of resolve. "And Tom?"

"Yes, ma'am?"

"You are safe. I promise, no one will ever hurt you again."

"No, ma'am. They won't."

IT WAS LATE IN THE day when Mary explained she had to go to work at Henry's diner. She knew I'd be fine without her, she said, and took me to the living room to show me the "TV." It was what I'd seen in one of the windows when I first got to the city: moving miniature people inside a box. Mary explained how to change the channels and adjust the volume, and served me dinner before she left for her shift. She also said that while she was at work she and Henry would talk about what to do with me, and that if I was still awake when she returned, we'd discuss it then.

I was sitting on that green couch watching men in

suits talk and talk and talk as she turned the key in the front door's lock. While I had been locked up before, I don't think I knew what lonely was until I actually had someone to miss. And I missed Mary the second she left the room.

Television, however, offered some comfort. Those suited, talking men sat at desks and filled my small brain with information: an entire world of information that had been kept from me for so long. I was entranced by the small box, by all of it.

The miniature people spoke of wars, men killing each other over land, and showed images of children running half-naked through streets that didn't look like streets, terror in their eyes, pain on their faces, tiny bodies wracked with deformities only war can inflict. You know, son, for all I'd been through, I felt sorry for them. I still had the ability to feel for someone I'd never met. And this was something my own kin could never do—I'm pretty sure that when Grandpa was pinned under that truck my father never felt sorry for him. No, he was just angry about the interruption to his own schedule. He had things he wanted to get done—and taking his father to the doctor wasn't one of them. There was nothing in it for him. He felt only for himself.

Thankfully empathy was attached to a gene my father did not pass on to me. When I saw those children run, I felt for them. I didn't know why, but

I wished they weren't suffering. I suppose, like Mary, I really couldn't understand how people could do this kind of thing to children.

The news was interrupted from time to time by other people trying to tell me to spend money on cars, soap and bigger, better TVs. These people smiled a lot, and honestly, they did make me want to buy their soap and cars.

Later, I watched several shows that seemed to be about what life was like with "normal" families. In those worlds fathers wore clean white shirts and ties at dinner and their children ate with them at the same table. On some shows the families had three boys; on some a girl and a boy; and on others, three girls and three boys. One thing was constant in these families: they all had a mother, and she was always well-dressed, pretty and caring. She always listened to whatever problems the kids had.

Now understand, son, I had no idea what TV really was or that these were not real families. In all seriousness, I believed I was watching *real* families in *real* situations. How could I know that these "problems" had been some writer's creation? How could I know that no family is ever as perfect as those I watched? There was a point in the evening where I wondered if they could see me. Or worse, whether someone out there was watching my life unfold in a tiny box in their living room.

These thoughts didn't consume me, however. The families did. I watched sons come to their fathers with questions about girls, money and school. I was amazed when these men with huge white teeth sat down and treated their boys with dignity, respect and love. They put hands on their shoulders when they spoke with them. They didn't frown at them, hit them or hold their faces to a hot stove. To me, these fathers seemed unreal. And in truth, they were. But when you consider it truthfully, they were a lot closer to real than my father. It's not one of those "somewhere in the middle" things; no, he was at one end of the father chart, and they were at the other. I wished I had a dad who was at the other end of the spectrum. Most men are somewhere near it—maybe not all the way, but pretty damn close. Very few are at the same end as my father, thank God, and little man, as I write this to you, I pray that when I am judged, I am placed closer to the TV men.

I have had some good influences, son, and I believe they've helped me be a better father to you. And yes, some of them were actually from TV. As unrealistic as they may have been, they were what I aspired to—I wanted to be the clean, white-shirted, tie-wearing man at the head of the table, telling your mother how good dinner was and listening to your problems, giving advice with the wisdom of my age. Believe me, I'm truly sorry, but I did try.

Darkness overcame the fall evening quickly and dark hands grabbed the room as well. The only safe thing was the TV. The box lent warmth to the room. Changing scenes made light dance across the walls, furniture and pictures. Every once in a while, there was total blackness—it was always over quickly, but always a little scary. My fears disappeared as soon as some smiley-faced person appeared, telling me to drink this coffee or use that cleaner.

I watched for hours on end until I finally I lay back on the couch and fell into a deep, restful sleep. I still, on occasion, like to fall asleep in front of the television. There's something comforting about hearing voices in the background as you sleep. It's kind of like someone is in the room with you, watching over you. A false sense of security—I know—but a false sense of security is better than no security at all.

The box, I learned later in life, is the only friend some people have. They rarely interact with others. Maybe they go out to get food, buy the things their smiling "friends" are telling them to buy, but they always return to their own living rooms, to the warm glow and comforting voices coming from their TV. They don't have drama in their lives, so they lose themselves in the lives of the people they watch. They laugh with them, cry with them, love with them, and some even believe they are them. They waste the time they could be spending living life watching the lives of others.

Son, are these people all that different than I was in my youth? Are they alive? Do they make choices? Are they not as much a slave to the box as I was to my father? I think, on some level, it's the same thing. Their jail is just a whole lot more comfortable than mine ever was.

STATIC HAD FILLED the screen when I woke to hear the squeal of the door's hinges and realized that Mary was home. The kitchen light was turned on, and it sent a glow down the hallway. I heard the whispers of voices and knew that Henry had returned with Mary.

They walked down the hall and stood in the doorway to the living room, silhouetted by the kitchen light. They didn't speak—just two shadows checking to see if I was still there. I stirred so they could see I was awake.

"Tom, you're still up?" Mary spoke softly.

"Yes, ma'am. I did fall asleep though." Groggy, I got to my feet slowly.

"How are you, Tom?" Henry asked.

"I'm fine, sir."

"Do you want to come to the kitchen for a snack? Henry and I were just going to make sandwiches."

"Yes, ma'am."

At the kitchen table, Henry eyed me up and smiled.

"You look like a million bucks, son."

Mary beamed at the compliment.

"A million bucks, sir?"

"Ah, it means you look great, Tom. Really great. Mary, you fixed him up real good. Real good."

"Yes, sir. Thank you, sir. Mary got me some clothes and cut my hair."

"I see that, Tom. Well, son, you are a handsome young man. Isn't he, Mary?"

She ran her fingers through my hair and said, "He sure is. A real fine young man."

I still get chills about that moment as I write this to you. She had a genuine affection for me. Just as I had for her. Henry could see this as well and smiled; pleased, it seemed, he'd convinced Mary to take me home.

"Tom, are you okay to sit a bit and talk, or did you want to go to bed?" Henry asked.

"I'm okay. I'm not tired no more."

"Well, that's great, son. Are you hungry, Tom? I'm starved. You'd think running a diner I'd always be full, but no sir, I don't hardly get time to have a smoke, let alone sit and eat a meal. Mary, get the boy a sandwich. You like sandwiches, Tom? How 'bout pickles, Mary, and milk? Grab the boy a glass of milk. Everyone knows a growing boy needs milk. You like milk, Tom? What kinda meat you like? Ham? Beef? I think I brought Mary some turkey last week. Mary, you got any turkey?"

"Take a breath, Henry, and let Tom answer—you're prattling on like a schoolgirl."

"I just want to be sure the boy gets some food, that's all. He needs to get some meat on his bones. That all, Mary. That's all."

"I know, Henry, I know. You're a sweet man." She leaned in and kissed him on the top of his forehead.

"Not in front of Tom, Mary, please."

"Oh, Henry . . ." she said, winked, and then walked to the fridge.

By this time, Mary understood the limits of my experience and offered to let me taste both the mustard and the mayo before putting them on my sandwich. I liked the mustard—it woke up my mouth. She piled meat on homemade bread, cut it in half, placed it on a plate with a pickle and dropped it in front of me. She did the same for Henry and then herself. I waited for her because Henry waited for her. She finally sat after pouring a glass of beer for Henry, and milk for me and for herself.

"Go ahead, Tom. You can eat now," Henry said while he crunched on a dill. "Mary, you make the best pickles. Wow, this is good."

"Henry, please don't talk while you're chewing. I'm trying to teach this young man some manners and you're going to undo it all in one meal."

"I'm sorry, Mary. Tom . . . but you know, on your feet all day . . . and these pickles . . . Go ahead, Tom.

Try that pickle. Best you'll ever eat. If only I could get her to make 'em for the diner, well, sir, I'd be rich. She won't, though. No, sir. She won't. Doesn't want to turn pickling into a job. Says she likes it too much. Doesn't want to ruin it for herself—that's something, isn't it, Tom? She loves it so much she doesn't want to do it. That's a good one!"

A sideways glance from Mary changed Henry's course.

"Look at me, Tom, doing all the talking. And about pickles. You don't care about pickles, do you? Of course you don't. You've had quite a couple of days, haven't you? So what do you think, Tom? Are you okay? Feeling better?"

He finally stopped to take a bite of his sandwich and wash it down with a gulp of golden beer.

"So, Tom, tell me." He paused. "How are you?"

I waited, not sure if Henry was going to let me answer before firing another question at me.

"I'm fine, sir," I finally said. "Mary's been real nice. She showed me the toilet. It's not gold, you know. Let me take a shower. And gave me a warm dress to sleep in."

I'm not sure if it was the gold toilet or the warm dress that caused Henry to start coughing, but cough he did. Mary and I watched as he covered his mouth with one hand and held up the other. A chubby index finger pointed to the sky as he regained his composure, took a sip of beer and said, "What? Gold? Dress?"

117

I tried to speak, but Mary beat me to it.

"Shush, Henry. I explained the toilet to him and he had to sleep in something so I gave him one of my flannel nightgowns. He didn't mind."

"Well, he didn't mind being called *Boy* either, but that don't make it right. A boy, I mean, a young man, don't sleep in no nightgown. Mary, you gotta get this . . . lad some proper pajamas, something suitable for a young man . . ."

"It's already done, Henry. You can relax. Here, I'll get you another beer. You poor thing, I thought you were going to choke to death."

"I almost did. You shouldn't do that to a man, shock him half to death."

"Oh, you'll live," she said, patting his back and placing a full glass of beer in front of him.

"Thank you, Mary. You're a good woman."

"It's nice to hear you say it in front of somebody else for a change."

"Please don't start, Mary. Not in front of Tom."

"I'm just playing with you, Henry. Just playing."

He sat back in his chair, pushed his now empty plate away and said, "I know you are, Mary. I know. And you *are* a good woman."

She smiled again, but only at Henry.

There was more to this moment than I could have known, son. But when I look back at it, it's a very clear window into what was an unconventional, but loving, relationship. I was glad they shared it with me; as uncomfortable as it may have been for them, it taught me how to love them even more. While I thought Mary was perfect, I could sense that even she was somehow flawed. What the flaw was, I didn't know—but it still made her seem more human, more real . . . more perfect.

You see, son, it's the people who are not afraid to show their flaws who are often the most loveable. It's those, like the people in the TV families, who seem to have no flaws, or warts or whatever you want to call them, who may not even be likeable. Mary and Henry showed me it's okay to be flawed, and even more okay to let people know you are flawed. When you display your warts or scars, you don't have to spend much time covering them up—you can actually spend your time doing more important things, like laughing and loving. I really believe this, son, and so should you. Life is a lot easier when you're not hiding who are. I suppose this is one of the reasons I am writing you this letter—I want you to see my flaws. I want you to know who I really am. I am a man of many, many warts. Ugly ones.

"TOM," HENRY CONTINUED, "we have to talk to you. You know, about what we are going to do . . . with you."

I straightened up in my chair the way a child does when they are included in a serious conversation.

"This is a very strange situation we find ourselves in, Tom. Odd, if you will. I mean, who would've imagined, two days ago, you wandering into our lives. All I was doing was taking a break and having a smoke, and there you were. My God, you were a mess. . . ."

"Henry!"

"I'm just sayin', he was a mess, Mary. He knows he was a mess. I'm not saying anything he don't know. Anyways, there you were, a scared little rabbit: and here you are now, all cleaned up and, you know, Tom, thank God I took my break when I did, because who knows what woulda happened. Who knows where you'd be if we didn't find you? God, I hate to even think about it. It can be a mean city out there, Tom. Mean and cold."

He stopped.

"Thank God, sir," I mimicked.

"Well, Tom, we did find you, and you're safe. With us . . . with Mary. Yes, sir, she took real good care of you. Real good. As good as any mother would her own son."

He looked at Mary as though he'd said something he shouldn't have. She looked away.

He took a drink of beer and continued. "The thing is, Tom, what do we do? We can't go to the law, Mary's explained that. You won't go? 'Course you won't, and I don't blame you. Half the cops in this damn town are worse than the criminals. No, we can't go to the cops. So, me and Mary here, well, we're just simple people. Busy lives and all. And we ain't sure just how to solve this problem. Not that you're a problem, Tom, 'cause you ain't. No, you just present a problem. One that's gotta be solved real quick. I mean, me and Mary, we can't be running around town buying boys' clothes and such. People, well, people know us. We've been here our whole lives. They know we don't got kids. How do we explain that? How do we explain Mary buying twice as much food? And what about you, Tom? You gotta go outside at some point. A man needs sunlight. Otherwise he turns yellow. No, you gotta be able to go out, run, play, get some exercise. You're a young man. A young man has to exercise. He'd get all flabby like me if he don't. I never got no exercise—always working at the diner with my dad, since I was younger than you. Then my dad—well, one day he drops dead in the diner, right at the lunch rush. . . . They wheel him out and I keep putting orders on the counter. I closed up for two hours the day of the funeral and made it back for the dinner rush. But that's nothing to you, Tom. Just letting you know, you gotta get outside, burn the flab off."

He rubbed his belly lightly overtop of his shirt, then continued, "Not that you got any flab, but you would if you were stuck in a diner eighteen hours a day. So anyways, Tom, see, Mary and me, we got this problem, and we wanted to talk to you about it before we made a decision. You know, get your thoughts on this thing. See what were gonna do. But with your help."

I sat motionless, desperately wanting to understand just what Henry was really saying. I kind of understood that I posed a problem, but I'd never really thought about what would happen next. My great plan never jumped that far ahead. I had to get away; I did that. What came next—well, that never crossed my mind. It was pretty clear to me now that I probably wasn't going to shit in a gold toilet and that I probably could not survive long in a cold, mean city without help.

"Sir?"

"Yes, Tom."

"I don't want to cause problems. I'm sorry."

"No, no, Tom," Mary said, "you're not a problem." She reached across the table and grabbed my hand, giving Henry a stern look. "It's the situation that is the problem. Not you. You didn't cause this, Tom. Don't ever feel that way. Don't ever feel you're a problem."

"Oh sure, Tom, heck no. You're not the problem. It is the situation. You see, eighteen hours a day in a diner don't give a man much time to learn how to explain himself real well. You see, Tom, it would be easy for Mary and me just to call the cops or child services and hand you over. Well, then, we'd never have to see you again and we could go on with our lives like you were never here. But Tom . . ." He became very serious then, staring into my eyes. "Me an' Mary, well, we ain't like that. We wouldn't throw you to the curb like an old bag a trash. 'Cause you ain't, Tom, you ain't trash. No sir. You're a human being. And human beings, well, most ain't trash. And you definitely ain't trash. No, sir, me and Mary, well, we want to figure this thing out. One way or another, we, the three of us, sitting here, we *are* going to figure this out. And not just what's best for Mary and me, but what's best for you, Tom. You understand that? Tom, do you understand we want what's best for you? To protect *you*?"

"Yes, sir. I think I do."

And I think I did. I could tell they cared for me, even though they had known me for less than two days. And I cared for both of them now too—Mary for the way she touched my hand at just the right moment, and Henry for the way that he struggled to explain he cared. It was awkward, but beautiful.

"You see, Tom, and I don't mean to scare you, but Mary and me, well, we can't, well, you can't . . ." He struggled for words.

Mary put her hand on Henry's—he was fighting the lump.

"Tom, son, what Henry is trying to say is that we can't keep you here long," Mary said quietly. "It's not that we don't want you here. God knows the past two days, looking after you, well, it's been . . . well, it's been just wonderful. You see, Tom, Henry and I, we've never had kids of our own, and having you here, well it's been just like having a son of my . . . of our own. It really is special, Tom. You're special."

I suppose I must have looked emotionless; I just sat quiet and listened, not needing or wanting to say a word. For a while, the only sound in the room was the hum of the old refrigerator.

"Tom, I got a sister. A real good woman. A good woman like Mary here. And her husband, well, there ain't never been a better man in the whole world. Well, Tom, I called them today. You see, they got kids and they're real good with kids. They know all about them, and their clothes, and their music, and school and stuff. And well, Tom, they got this big ol' house, and room and well . . ."

It was like when someone is trying to tell you they've got cancer and they're dying, but that you will be fine without them. They don't believe it any more than you do, but you both pretend.

"I spoke with her too, Tom," Mary picked up. "You see, we are too close to where you grew up. If someone starts asking questions, well, they could end up here and none of us wants that. We want to protect you, Tom. Keep you safe."

Her large dark eyes searched for my approval, something, anything to indicate that I understood and wasn't hurt by them trying to pass me on to someone else. The thing is, as much as I loved them both and would have spent the rest of my life with them, I understood. I really did. My desire to distance myself from my grandfather and father—as far as possible—was greater than my desire to stay with Mary and Henry.

"I understand," I said. "I want to be far away, too. And if you think I'm not far enough, I need to keep going."

Their surprise was palpable. It seemed convincing me hadn't been as difficult as they feared.

"You've both been so good to me. 'Specially you, Mary. But I don't want them to find me. Ever." I stopped for a moment, then wondered aloud: "Do you think your sister'll help me, sir? I don't want to be no bother to no one. I could go on my own if I had to."

"Tom," Mary said, "you will never have to go on your own again. Least not while I'm breathing."

"While we're breathing, Tom," Henry said.

"You have to understand, Tom," Mary continued, "we're not abandoning you. We're just getting you somewhere safer than this. Tom, they could be looking for you right now. God knows what they might do if they found you. I mean, look at what they've done already."

She looked down at her hands, fighting back tears

again. Not tears of sadness this time, tears of anger.

For a moment, I wasn't worried what they might do to me, but what Mary might do to them. Henry spoke next.

"I talked with my sister, Tom. I told her what I know about you, which ain't much, but enough to understand you need help in a bad way. A real bad way." He took a sip of beer and swallowed. "She's a good woman, Tom, a real fine person. Well, I didn't even finish the story with her, and, well, she knew where I was going and asked when I was bringing you to meet her. That's just the way she is, Tom."

"I'll visit you whenever I can, Tom," Mary said. "Whenever I can."

"I know you will, Mary. I know." She would— we had established a bond that would only become stronger in the distance between us. Somehow, I just understood that Mary would always be with me. She related in a way that was beyond what even some mothers feel for their sons. It was both strange and eternal. I felt the same way towards her. And I never doubted, not even for a second, that she meant what she said.

Mary began to clear the dishes and Henry polished off his beer with a relieved last gulp. I watched both of my new friends and knew everything was going to be fine. If I wanted to stay, I know they would have agreed. Still, I knew leaving was for the best.

Henry gave Mary a warm hug and patted me on the shoulder before leaving. It was the same kind of physical gesture the TV fathers gave their sons.

MARY TUCKED ME IN once more, kissed my forehead and said three words I'd never heard before: "I love you." I didn't really understand them then, but my eyes well up as I write them down now. Sleep came fast and easy. I sank into the bed with thoughts of the future and its possibilities: new people, a new city or town, a new house.

And, finally, I wasn't afraid.

ARRANGEMENTS WERE MADE and new clothes packed. Two days later I was taking my second ride in a car, half-hidden in the backseat by clothes, some other supplies and a cooler. It would be a five-hour drive, Henry said, and we'd stop for a picnic. Mary had prepared some salads, fried chicken and her world-famous pickles.

Driving in broad daylight produced a whole new set of sensations for me, and Henry, the eager tour guide, watched me in the rearview mirror, pointed out sights and vehicles and gave me a lesson in the history of the highway.

"These were only two-lane gravel roads when I was

a kid, Tom. Now look at it. Everybody's in such a rush to get to where they're goin' they miss the trip. You see, Tom, getting there is most of the fun. Look at that rig coming up behind us, Tom. Man, he must be going eighty. Lord, I stick to fifty-five miles per hour, Tom. No sir, no ticket for me. And with the price a gas these days, well, fifty-five, that's the best speed. Here she comes, Tom. Look at that thing."

As the semi powered by, the car shook. Henry, both hands on the wheel, never skipped a beat. "That's a transport, Tom. They carry freight from one end of the country to the other. That one's handling fuel. You'd think he'd be more careful. Boy, if that thing went up there wouldn't be nothing left of that rig." He went on like this for hours. Mary tried to quiet him down, but I found the information useful.

We stopped at a rest area, used the washrooms, ate and got back on the road.

"How you feeling, Tom? Nervous?" Mary asked, wanting me to know it would only be normal if I was.

"I'm fine, ma'am. A little nervous, I guess, but fine, thanks."

"You'll do just great. Jim and Liz, well, they'll love you just like we do."

"They sure will, Tom," Henry said. "You're a good lad. You'll settle in with those folks real well."

We drove a couple more hours and were nearing the end of the journey when Henry said, "Tom, we're almost at Jim and Liz's now. It's real important you don't tell no one where you're from. Remember, you're a cousin from outta town. Your parents died in a car accident. Don't tell nobody anything else. The kids don't know nothing about you, just that you need a place to live. Okay, Jim and Liz, they know, but they won't say nothing to nobody. You understand, Tom?"

"Yes, sir. I won't say anything else."

"Good boy."

With that, the town came into view. It was much smaller than the city we'd left and it sat on the shores of a small lake. I didn't know it at the time, but it was one of those towns where no one said anything about anyone—but still, everyone knew everything about everyone. There was a quiet acceptance of a boy like me: one who did not share the last name of the people he lived with. As it turned out, I was not the only cast-off living with relatives.

In this place, "nieces and nephews" were raised by grandparents, uncles and aunts or old family friends. It was still typical, in those days, to send a child away when his or her mother was unmarried. There was always an explanation, not unlike mine—and as I said, quiet acceptance. People whispered in low tones while sharing a pot of tea or over a beer, but no one ever came out and asked you. It was the perfect place for me.

We meandered through the quaint streets until we came to a large red-brick home across from the lake. Boats were put up for the winter but you could imagine its summer beauty: people laughing, sitting on their docks in the warm evening; boats bobbing; children splashing at the shore or jumping off rafts.

The house had a large white porch and my new family was seated outside, waiting for their new arrival. As we pulled into the gravel drive, they got up to greet us at the porch steps.

"How are you, Henry?" The men shook hands.

"Oh, Mary, it's so good to see you!" The women embraced.

Everyone became quiet, then turned to me. Mary broke the silence cautiously. "Jim, Liz, this is Tom. Tom, this is Jim and Liz."

Jim stuck out his hand. I'd watched the men do this, so I stuck out mine. "It's real nice to meet you, Tom."

"It sure is, Tom," said Liz.

I said it was real nice to meet them too.

It was awkward; I'm not going to lie to you, son. I mean, here I was, a boy none of them knew anything about standing in their driveway, and they were taking me in. Henry, whether intentionally or not, broke the ice in a way only Henry could.

"By God, Jim, it's been a long drive. I gotta use the head."

The adults laughed. Mary gave Henry a disapproving look. Henry responded with one that meant "What'd I say?"

Regardless, I think we were all grateful, and idle chatter began. Jim led Henry inside to the washroom while Mary and Liz began catching up on gossip. Together, we walked towards my new home.

And what a home it was: not extravagant, but impressive. The main floor rooms were large, nicely decorated and friendly. I say friendly because while it was all very nice, a person wouldn't be afraid to come in and sit on the sofa or at the wooden table in the kitchen. Even though I'd never been there, there was a sense of warm familiarity, an atmosphere that said, "Come in, take your shoes off and sit." Of course, at that point I don't think I could articulate this, but the years I spent there, watching people come in and out, taught me to appreciate it.

Liz and Mary took me upstairs to my new room. The second floor was surprisingly large, with rooms shooting off in all directions. Mine was at the end of the hall, next to a second-storey door that led to nothing but a twenty-foot drop. I suppose there was going to be a balconey there at some point, but I don't know, I never asked. It seemed normal to everyone else, and in time I guess I pretended to know what everyone else knew. Maybe they didn't know any more than I did. People are strange that way. They will go along with something as long as everyone else is.

My room had a bed, a window and a large chest

of drawers. There was no closet. The paint on the walls was a faded blue that made the room feel cool regardless of the temperature. We put away my few belongings in the chest. I think we barely filled three of the nine drawers of the old wooden cabinet. The one item that wasn't put away was the sundress. I kept that folded in my pocket. Mary didn't ask; I didn't tell.

Liz showed me the bathroom and the master bedroom she and Jim shared, should I need them. Then we went back downstairs. Henry and Jim were having a beer and talking quietly and intensely.

The creaky old stairs warned of our imminent arrival, and they immediately changed the tone of their discussion.

"Whatta ya think?" Henry asked, smiling to flash the few teeth he had left.

"It's fine, sir."

"See, what'd I tell ya, Mary? The boy'll be fine. It's a real nice place ya got here, Jim. A real nice place." He took a swig of beer, but didn't leave enough room for anyone else to speak. "Why, a man'd give his right arm to live in a place like this. Big house, lotsa yard out back, a lake out front. Yes, sir, I might move in with you next. A real nice home. Definitely. Real nice."

I don't know who he was trying to convince: me, Mary or himself.

If I've learned anything about Henry over the years, it's that dropping me off with his sister was as hard on him as it was on Mary. It's just that men of that era weren't allowed to show their emotions. Mary, of course, tried to explain, but even she couldn't have gotten into Henry's head at that very moment. Sitting here, writing to you, I think I understand. I just wish I understood sooner.

Liz finally took over. "Tom, we are sure you will be very happy here, too. And thank you, Henry, we like to think it is a very nice home." She looked at me as she spoke, and concentrated on Mary. I really think Mary needed more assurance than I did; I mean, she'd met me not even a week earlier, and here she was dropping me off for someone else to raise. Despite the fact that I was not her flesh and blood, I believe that in those few days, those precious moments, we became mother and child. She felt it; I felt it. And to this day I still feel it. When people ask, "Who is your mother?" I always answer the same way: "Her name is Mary."

"You know, Tom," Jim said, "we need to talk about our situation."

"Yes, sir."

He was more formal than Henry, more like the fathers I had seen on TV. He chose his sparing words carefully.

"Let's sit," he said. And we did.

We reviewed the story they'd given people; I was reminded that this was a small town and that people liked to talk. There will be questions, I was told; I must have answers. They had spoken briefly to their kids, who were intentionally sent out prior to my arrival, and they too knew what to say. They were told precious little, actually, to prevent them from being tripped up by curious neighbors—you can't tell a lie if you don't know you're lying. As far as the kids knew, I really was a distant cousin whose parents had been killed in a car wreck.

I am the only one that knows the real story. And now, I am telling it to you, son. Sometimes things need to come to a boil before they spill out completely. Tonight, things came to a boil.

I GUESS YOU'D SAY I adapted well to living with Jim and Liz. Besides, what option did I have? There was a tearful goodbye when Mary and Henry finally left that day, mostly on Mary's part—but not completely. I felt sad myself, but I didn't cry.

Jim and Liz had three daughters and a son. The boy, Zach, was the oldest. He was leaving for college in a year and eventually proved to be a great role model for me. In fact, it was probably Zach's influence that's allowed me to write this letter. He was the one who took the time to teach me to read and to write. Liz and Jim couldn't send to me school that first year. The story was that I was too sick to attend—that I would enroll the next fall. The truth was, I had much to learn before I could even dream of going to school.

That first winter, Zach sat with me for hours on end, teaching me. In fact, he taught me to the point that I could read and write better than most of the kids in my grade.

The girls—Theresa, Sarah and Stephanie—well, they simply doted on me. Sure, they helped with my schooling too, but they were so motherly you'd swear I was their child.

Normally, the "new kid in town" novelty wears off pretty quick and then people begin to treat you like everyone else. Well, that wasn't the case with those girls and me. I can't tell for sure if they saw a lifetime's pain on my face, in my eyes, or whatever, but they never stopped fawning. God help kids who even thought about teasing me in the schoolyard. I'll tell you, son, kids in small towns can be just as tough and mean as kids in large towns or cities. And a lot of the kids around there earned rock-hard muscles baling hay, feeding cattle and slaughtering hogs. And yes, my little man, if a boy like that wanted a piece of you, he took it.

I rarely felt the bullies' wrath, mostly because the girls would have none of it. But when one or more of them did challenge me, they never could hurt me: as strong as they were, none could hit as hard as my father.

My reputation grew. I was a quiet boy who never fought back, but I also never showed I could be hurt.

After a while, they rarely challenged me, leaving me alone to read, eat my lunch or whatever else.

THE YEARS FLEW BY quickly, living with Liz and Jim. I grew and I matured most like every other boy in town. It turned out I was a pretty good student—I could comprehend almost anything they threw at me. Parched for so long, I had a thirst for knowledge and enjoyed learning anything new. I read every book I could get my hands on, and while I was quiet, I was not shy about asking questions in the classroom. I felt that if the teacher was there to teach, I might as well stay on a subject until I completely understood it. Some teachers liked me for that—others clearly wanted to get home to their backyard and a martini.

I suppose the other kids had little use for my questions, but I wasn't there for them. And hell, the truth is half of them probably wanted to ask the same questions anyway. The other half? Well, they probably couldn't formulate a question if their lives depended on it.

From grade school to high school this continued. And ultimately, it was the same in college.

No, I wasn't the most popular kid, but then again, I really wasn't the most unpopular. I bet if I didn't ask so many questions, the other students wouldn't have even known I existed. At times, mostly outside of the classroom, I was invisible. And that was fine with me—I didn't crave attention like some kids do. I was pretty comfortable with who I was, and as a result, I didn't feel the need to act like a jackass. When you think about where I came from, it's hard to believe: I was probably better adjusted than many of the other students.

Son, I don't want you to think I was one of those lonely, brooding artist types who intentionally become different—the kind that seem to want to be left alone, but do it in such a way that it seems like they want everyone to watch them be different and alone. Those guys are really just screaming for attention, criticizing mainstream culture, turning up their noses at everyone outside their own sub-society.

That wasn't me; I just was. I went about my business, had few friends and even fewer girlfriends. It's not that I wasn't attracted to girls or them to me. It's just that I felt awkward. Somehow I always wanted them to be the perfect combination of Mary and the girl in the brown sundress.

Yes, I still thought and dreamed about her often.

The dreams became less violent and more loving. She grew up in my fantasy as I grew up in real life. Amazingly, as I became a man, she became a woman. I fell in love with her over and over again. I could feel her touch, smell her hair, enjoy her embrace, but never hear her speak. She had been silenced long ago and no dream could bring that back. She'd been muted, forever. Until tonight, that is.

Girls fascinated me as much as I did them. They were a challenge to most of the boys in school, while I was a challenge of a different sort. They were used to snapping their fingers and any number of guys would come running. Me? I couldn't be bothered. This was unacceptable, unbelievable to most of them. Some tried to lure me, others looked at me in disgust—as though I were some sort of an alien for not knowing how special they were. And when someone's told they're special their whole life . . . well, it's not good.

Honestly, we are all special to someone. But we're not special to everyone. You are special to me, but the six billion others on the planet are not likely to be as amazed with your smile as I am.

I was special to Mary, but to the other kids at school, I was just another guy in jeans and a T-shirt. These girls, however, and some of the guys, thought everyone else on the planet should treat them just like their mommy or daddy—and a storm blew through if they didn't. They had no time for anyone who didn't kiss their butts when, in truth, those were the only people they should have been listening to.

Time is the great equalizer. I've seen the beauty queen of ninth grade at twenty-nine: she should have chosen her friends more carefully. The star high school football quarterback has lost his hair, squeezes himself into extra-large shirts and sorts nuts and bolts in a factory. If I can give some advice—and that's what I am doing tonight—remember, you are an adult a lot longer than you're a teen. High school is a four-year popularity contest. Life is life.

I finished college with an honors degree in history and a minor in literature. As I've told you, I loved books growing up, son, and those two subjects meant a lot of reading.

Maybe someday, if a forensic psychologist reads this, they'll write, "He used books as an escape from the pain of his early childhood." Many others will agree—and honestly, so would I. I was constantly losing myself in someone else's life. I think we all do it, at one time or another. Reading, we escape to a place no one has ever really been, or can ever go to again. I majored in that in college, and that's okay. Because while I was escaping, I was learning. Too many others were escaping and not getting a damn thing out of it.

For me, college was an uneventful four years. I stayed in touch with Mary and Henry, and Liz and Jim and the family.

I was in my third year when Mary called with the news of Henry's death.

At first, all she said was my name, "Tom . . ." and already I knew what had happened. I cried—the only time I had since I escaped the farm.

At first I tried to swallow it—the lump. My thoughts took me back to the farm—as though it was yesterday. The punches, the kicks, as fresh as the day I left. And then I looked around me: I was in *my* room, on the phone with the woman I called my mother. . . . Suddenly it was okay to let the lump out.

We talked for hours, the tears rolling down my cheeks like an August thunderstorm. Ultimately those tears helped us come to terms with the death of the greatest man I've ever met.

He died at the counter, you know. Just like his dad. He would have wanted it that way.

Mary and I joked that because I was the closest thing to Henry's son that I should return and run his diner. But finishing my degree, she knew, was too important to me—and Henry would have wanted that too. . . . A restaurant was definitely out of the question.

Henry left Mary the diner—which she sold— some other property and enough life insurance that she could quit working and spend her last years in lonesome comfort.

Mary could have moved to a bigger place and still have had money in the bank, but that wasn't the way she was. She didn't have to work for the diner's new owners, but she still did her regular shifts for her regular customers. She was as much a fixture as the counter and the stools. I know how her customers felt: Mary never let me down. If she wasn't working she was home to answer the phone and listen to my problems. She rarely judged, but I knew when she was reverting to the "sundress" state of mind.

We spoke every week and she did as well as can be expected without her soulmate. I never asked why they didn't marry; she never said. It was one of those things I simply accepted as a part of their unconventional relationship. It worked for them and that was all that mattered. I can also tell you that there was never a couple who cared more for one another. If my teachers taught me how to learn, Mary and Henry taught me how to love. And by love I mean unconditionally. They taught me to love the way I love you.

I don't expect anything from you, son. Not even love. I would actually understand if you didn't love me. I love you because I do, because I can't help it. When I look at you lying in that chair, shadows dancing across you, I almost can't contain myself. I want to pick you up, feel your small arms around me, your tiny face nuzzled into my neck, your heart beating against mine. But I can't—I leave you be to finish this. That's the type of love Henry and Mary had. Neither one loved the other because they had to. They just loved—because they wanted to.

I wouldn't say Mary and I got closer after Henry's death. I'm not sure that was possible, anyway. But we did talk a little more, and about more things. More about her, in particular. I gave advice on certain things and she took it. We never talked about how she and Henry came into my life—it was ancient history, and it didn't matter. I was her confidant, and she mine. I could tell her anything.

The only time this was tested was when girls came up. None was good enough in Mary's eyes. Inadvertently, I'd discovered her only real flaw. Her Tom was very close to perfect—and the girls trying to woo him were not. I think many mothers go through this with their sons. It only proved that, as saintly as she was, Mary was human.

And I love the human Mary as much, and maybe more, than the saintly Mary. As I've told you before, it is often our flaws that make us most endearing. I don't know why; it just is.

I GRADUATED COLLEGE and stayed on as a teaching assistant with every intention of getting a Masters and Ph.D. in either history or literature. I worked under several profs and helped teach several classes for a number of years, but mostly I enjoyed a simple life of reading, teaching and being.

I followed no real timetable, had no strong desire to finish and get out into "the real world," no need to live beyond my means or waste time chasing down the Joneses. My apartment was simple; my car decent but dented. I had no attachments.

And then I met her, son. Your mother.

My life would never be the same. It was good; it was

bad; at times it was great. Since the girl in the brown sundress, no woman had affected me this way. There are perfectly stunning women who just don't captivate you the way others do. There has to be something more, let's call it charisma, to really entrance you.

This is not to say your mother wasn't beautiful; she was. She just wasn't what you might call a classic beauty. Actually, she was more on the cute side. And for my money? I'd take cute over outwardly beautiful any day of the week.

Now I'm not knocking beautiful women, but when the beauty fades—and it always does—there had better be that something else. If all you're going to do is stare at each other, well, that gets old in a hurry. You'd better have more in common.

Your mother and I had books.

I spent a lot of my time in the library. I couldn't afford to buy a new book every couple of days, so I'd go to the public library, sit in a corner and lose myself in the worlds of Steinbeck, Hemingway, Twain and Mitchell.

I first saw her carefully inspecting sections, looking for the one author or title that would catch her attention. It really was coincidental; normally I wouldn't have looked up from whatever book I might be devouring. I don't know what drew my attention, but I looked up just as one of the library's regulars was making his way towards her.

He was searching for titles in the same area, hoping to strike up a conversation with the tiny brown-haired bookworm.

You may find this hard to believe, son, but some men go to the library just to meet women. They even dress the part of the intellectual courtier—hell, if they were allowed, I'm sure they'd smoke a pipe.

That day I saw this cute, petite woman browsing, trying to sidestep the would-be Romeo. He wasn't taking the hint and made the near-fatal mistake of brushing up against her, not once, but three times in the span of about two minutes.

After the third "accident" she began a tirade that would've made a sailor blush. There weren't enough librarians in the whole county to silence her—and I couldn't turn away.

It was the first time a woman other than Mary or the girl in the sundress had my complete attention.

I don't remember much of what was said, but I admired the way this woman turned a grown man into a little boy. Her voice and demeanor let him know she was not backing down—that she was not beneath shoving one of the library's many books into a very uncomfortable place. He offered a meager apology and skulked away.

I was hiding behind a book when her still smoldering eyes found mine. She'd caught me now, too, but I couldn't look away. Hand on hips, she glared; I thought for sure I was next. Like an adolescent Peeping Tom, I was mesmerized and terrified at what might come at me.

I know it's a cliché, but time really did stand still. She had me there and then. There was no tirade, no explosion of books coming my way—just a smile, a nod and quick a turn down the aisle to head off in the same direction as her would-be suitor.

There are those who say love at first sight is a myth, that it just doesn't happen. Well, I loved your mother from that moment onward. She had a presence, something that demanded I get close, understand and, yes, love her. I'm probably not doing the best job of explaining, but I am not sure anyone else could do much better. Maybe that's why Mary never really said much about her and Henry—she couldn't. It was just one of those things. Why people are right for each other is sometimes just a mystery. Maybe it should remain that way.

Anyway, son, I was never the same. I sat in the library feeling elated and sad at the same time. I needed to see this woman again and speak with her, too, and didn't know if I ever would. What if she was a tourist or just passing through town visiting relatives? What if she never returned to my library again? How would I reconcile my feelings? I already had one ghostly girlfriend to contend with. I didn't think I could manage another.

For all I had been through, I'd never experienced anything like this. Mixed emotions were completely foreign to me. I was either happy or sad, sick or well, loving or hating. Now? Well, I was just plain confused. How could someone be so strong and aggressive and then three seconds later smile like that? I wasn't sure I'd ever know.

I tried to clear my mind and get back to my book, but it was no use. I kept coming back to the image of her smiling and then turning away; it was as if she was seeping into the pages I was trying to read. Thankfully, one of the librarians I knew quite well rescued me from my temporary purgatory.

"Tom?"

"Yes, Sandra?"

"This is a bit awkward for me, but I have a question for you."

"Sure."

"Did you see a young lady here a few minutes ago? Short, dark curly hair, dark eyes. . . ."

"What about her?"

"Well, she saw you. . . . And now, I'm no matchmaker, but I told her I'd give you her number and name, should you be interested."

"Number?" I sputtered.

"Well, yes, Tom. That's what young women of this generation do when they are interested. . . ."

No doubt she noticed me begin to blush.

"I see you here all the time, alone, reading, passing the days. Don't you think it's about time you found someone? Just take the number and think about calling." Sandra laughed, put a card down on the table in front of me and walked away.

It sat there for what seemed like an eternity. Finally I picked it up, turned it over and read the name.

Suzane. One *n*. Interesting, I thought.

I SUPPOSED I'D looked at that card a hundred times before I got home. Images of Suzane began evolving into imagined conversations. I paced around the apartment, rehearsing words, staring at the phone, looking out windows, searching for something that would either stop me from making the call or force me into finally dialing.

The whole thing was ridiculous. I knew I was going to call. How could I not?

She was adorable, and seemed to have the type of character I admire. I wasn't sure I had a "type" of woman—but if I did, she was definitely it. I do believe nature plays a big role in real attraction. I'm not talking about being attracted to nice clothes or a fancy car—that's not part of our real nature. Okay, sure, in today's society, it may be *natural,* but let's put it this way: it's not how God expected us to become attracted to one another.

No, we're supposed to be attracted to compatible partners. This isn't about race or religion, but when we were made we were programmed, somehow, to be attracted to those with the same fundamental values and beliefs. This is how we're supposed to keep the human race moving forward.

Actually, maybe a guy who is so interested in having a nice car attracting a woman who only likes guys with nice cars isn't really all that strange.

For me, son, it wasn't that I wanted to speak with this Suzane with one *n*—I needed to. I didn't have a choice: something in my genetic makeup forced my hand.

I probably dialed the number incorrectly the first three times. I dialed and didn't wait for an answer before I hung up. Then I realized that I was either leaving her—if I had dialed correctly—or some complete stranger extremely frustrated.

The fourth time, I hung in and let your mother answer. Each ring was agonizing. My heart pounded in my ears, I began to sweat and my tongue felt thick.

I wasn't sure I would even be able to speak to whoever picked up. I'm not sure what I was expecting when my call was finally answered, but there was a soft, gentle voice at the other end of the line. Maybe it was the library tirade, but when she answered, I was surprised by her friendly "Hello?"

The details are what they are: we spoke at length—

it must have been two hours—about everything and nothing. We never ran out of something else to say. There were no awkward pauses, no voids to fill. I had been on dates before, but now I had had my first intellectual, meaningful conversation with a woman I wanted to be with.

She was wonderful: funny, open and caring. We laughed at the tweed-jacketed library Casanova and wondered about the economy all within the first ten minutes.

She was as bright as she was adorable. Smart and sassy. I knew from the beginning this girl was approachable, but no pushover. No, son, your mother would be a challenge.

I was not only up to it, I welcomed the test. We had many dates: walking and talking in parks, going to the movies, dinners and yes, even a little dancing. And with each moment we spent together I fell deeper and deeper in love.

She was invitingly complicated. Soft, sweet and strong-willed at the same time, both vulnerable and stoic. She was alluringly awkward and magnificently imperfect.

That's why I loved her, son. She was flawed, wonderfully human.

She was like me. Like *us*.

We dated for a couple of months before I worked up the courage to take her to meet Mary. I had brought girls home before and it hadn't gone well. It never mattered all that much because I really didn't have anything invested in them. But Suzane—well, I was in love with her, and I'd told her as much. Truly loving someone other than Mary was strange and risky. I mean, how far would we get before she started asking questions about where I came from? About why Mary was so much older than a mother of someone my age should be?

But you know what, son? She never asked. That was another part of your mother's beauty. Suzane accepted me for me. Where I came from or how I got there didn't seem to matter. The only thing that was important to her was that I was there. *We* were there. Together.

We arrived at Mary's place on the same kind of fall weekend as when I first saw the lights of a city—cold, damp and, to most, depressing.

I didn't have the energy to think about it then, though. I was too nervous. I worried about Mary and I worried for Suzane. I should have known Suzane would hold her own. And really, I was the only one I needed to be nervous for: I was about to introduce the two strongest, most significant and amazing women I would ever know.

Well, my little man, I can tell you that all my apprehension was unfounded.

Mary immediately saw in Suzane what I saw in Suzane: strength, independence and true, meaningful beauty. I'm not sure if women have some kind of sixth sense about each other, but Mary loved your mother from the moment she sat at the very same chrome kitchen set where I'd had my first real haircut.

Mary's eyes were brighter, more alive than I'd seen in years; she drank in Suzane just as I first did. Your mother had a comfortableness that most people only dream about. A lot of folks actually pretend to have this type of energy—they hug you when they see you, they smile . . . but the moment you're gone, they're focusing on the negative. There was none of this, ever, son, in your mother or Mary. Good or bad, they told you. Hiding or holding in emotions was not a strong suit of either woman.

They recognized it as a common bond, I think. They talked endlessly in that kitchen, about this, that and other things I'm honestly not sure either one of them was really interested in. It didn't matter—they just enjoyed each other's company.

With that bridge crossed, son, your mother and I furthered our relationship. Like any couple, we had our differences, but by and large we were on the same page.

Again, this letter isn't for all the details, son, but I can assure you that your mother and I shared a loving relationship—one that was true and pure. And this, ultimately, led to your birth.

We spent four years together before she became pregnant. Four amazing, trying, wonderful years.

When we found out about you we were both ecstatic. Our love was growing beyond the two of us. We felt it even when you were in the womb, from the sound of your first heartbeat. We went to prenatal classes together and began mapping out our lives. We kept your ultrasound picture on the fridge until the day I drove your mother to the hospital.

I was going to stay on as a professor at the university—I was finally up for tenure—and your mother was going to stay home and raise our new family.

We got married very soon after we learned about the pregnancy. Mary was one of the few attendees; she smiled throughout.

Suzane was radiant. There's never been a more beautiful bride. Maybe I am biased, but why shouldn't I be?

My God, I loved her. She never quit. That is what made her so amazing. Her energy was eternal, like her smile, her spirit, her soul. Ongoing. Forever pleasing.

We were so excited about you. We decorated your nursery together, choosing neutral colors, decorations for either sex. We did not want to know which you were until the moment you were born.

There were sleepers and outfits neatly folded in drawers, diapers on hand, bottles in endless supply. We were armed and ready for you, little man. What we weren't ready for was your actual birth. You were early. Not real early, but early.

Not too early for us, certainly, but too early for the doctors. For some reason our doctor wasn't on call; there was an intern who had never delivered a child before on hand when I brought your mother in.

I don't know why they didn't call in a real doctor, but they didn't. Everything seemed fine: you mother glowing, your heart rate normal. I watched the news on the TV in the room.

Everything changed, utterly, in a flurry, son. Your heart rate dropped as you were ready to emerge. The moment changed from one of excitement to one of horror in the blink of an eye.

Your mother was screaming, nurses were scrambling, moving me out of the way and prepping your mother for the kind of birth I'm sure the intern wasn't qualified to perform.

Still, they did what they thought was right and got you out while your tiny heart was still beating.

Your mother, well, she was bleeding badly. It started during your birth and became worse after the rush of the procedure. Half of the nurses were trying to get you stabilized; the other half were trying to stabilize your mother.

As it turned out, the half that worked with you were more qualified. The others could not find a way to make your mother's bleeding stop. Suzane bled to death, not four feet from the both of us. There you were, new, bloody, beautiful, mine. And there she was: tired, bloody, beautiful—and then dead.

For the second time since I escaped the farm, I started to weep. I'm not sure I've stopped since.

Mary rescued me once more. I was a mess—honestly, I wasn't sure how I could go on. Within hours, Mary was there, supporting, instructing and advising. Thankfully she never gave me the chance to fall down. If I had fallen, I'm not sure I would've gotten up.

She never allowed me to feel weak, not Mary. Okay, she seemed to be saying, what next? How are you going to make this happen? How about that?

She would have made a great marine.

I'm not trying to paint Mary as cold; she was practical. Your mother had died and there wasn't anything I could do but grieve.

And the truth is, Mary loved your mother as much as I did. But she wouldn't allow herself to grieve as openly as I did. Did she do that that for me, or is that just how women of her generation were? I don't know. What I do know is that Mary never allowed me to make this tragedy about me.

She constantly reminded me about you and Suzane. She let me know, over and over again, that Suzane would have wanted you to be the one to survive if only one of you could live. She would also have wanted me to go on, pick myself up and raise our baby. Yes, *our* baby. Even though Suzane was gone, you were *ours*. A child born of love, nothing else. The fact that one of the people wasn't there anymore shouldn't change that.

Ultimately, it didn't.

I'm ashamed to admit that I'm glad, son, your mother isn't around tonight. I am positive she wouldn't have survived this.

As I've said, I never spoke to her about where I came from and she never asked. I was who I was. She was who she was. She may have had an incredible, terrible past too. But I never asked. And she never told.

I don't know if my nightmares ever woke her, or if she ignored them, meaning to ask about them "someday."

If she learned anything about my past during our many nights together, I suspect she died with that knowledge buried deep inside. It's probably just as well. I'm pretty sure she wouldn't have completely understood the fact that I still dreamed about a girl, now a woman, in a brown sundress.

That a girl maybe haunted me.

I don't know, or care.

What happened, happened—and I did nothing.

I was ten or maybe twelve, slack-jawed as I watched her be led away. I suppose—no, I've never supposed, I know—she was led to her death. What I didn't and couldn't know were the circumstances of her murder. I don't think I can be faulted for that. I was just a boy, barely that.

I had no power to stop anything, but why, why didn't I try?

THAT, MY SON, is really what has haunted me. Common sense might say that I was frozen by fear. Terrified about another beating—a life-threatening beating. But then I got one for not even trying to interfere anyway. No, son, I wasn't afraid of being punched or kicked. Beatings were nothing new to me.

But I honestly never knew what was going on in the mill. Honestly, I didn't.

At least not until this week.

Of course I guess I always suspected what the old men were doing. When I looked back at it. But I never *really* looked back. I spent years trying to put that life behind me after I met Henry and Mary, trying to pretend it never happened.

Does it make me as guilty as my pa and my grandpa for everything that has happened since?

I suppose. I'm not sure.

Do I have the blood of girls they took after I escaped on my hands? I burned down the mill, but left them the house.

I will say, to those girls, if were others: I am sorry. I will also say: tonight, you are avenged. There will be no more blood.

WHAT CHANGED? I did, son. I changed.

I'd been a widower for over five years, never enjoying the company of a woman since your mother. Never needed to—only focusing on you, your well-being, your needs and wants. I can't say whether it was pent-up desire or just plain old circumstance that brought us here tonight, but I can tell you, son, good or bad, I am glad for it.

Not two days ago, just after dropping you off at day care, I was driving my car down a street I'd driven a thousand times before. And that's when I saw her: blonde, brown-eyed and beautiful. She was about twelve, carrying a backpack, on her way to school without a care in the world.

I don't know what drew my attention other than I had nothing else on my mind. There she was—reminding me so much of the girl in the brown sundress that I almost believed it *was* her.

I circled the block, not sure what I was doing—knowing only that I *had* to talk to her. This should have been my first warning signal. In a few short moments, I had developed an obsession.

I needed to speak with this young girl.

Why did I? I don't know.

How would I? I didn't know that either.

I grew more excited as I drove, almost aroused as I saw her again. I slowed the car, pulling closer and closer to her walking along the sidewalk. I couldn't help myself. From behind her profile excited me as much as when I saw her from the front. Slight hips, hair falling to the middle of her back and floating in the breeze . . . just like the girl in the brown sundress.

I was sweating, thinking of what I would say—because I *was* going to approach her.

She was beautiful. For what reason, I don't know, but I knew I had to have her. I wanted to stroke her blonde locks; I wanted to hear her talk, feel her next to me.

I pulled up and rolled down the passenger side window.

I said something. She paused. She looked at me—a father, widower and son—and ran in horror. I'll never forget the look in her eyes—it was what I should have seen when the girl in the brown sundress was being led to the mill.

I sat there in my car, motionless, almost as horrified as she was. I remember looking in the rearview to see if anyone had watched this unfold. There was no one, but what I did see disgusted, terrified me.

The crazed green-yellow eyes I stared into did not belong to me. Son, they belonged to your grandfather. Just like that, I'd been transformed. In an instant I'd gone from a stable, productive member of society to an abomination.

I had become a monster.

My face was livid with rage, sweat dripped from

my brow, my features contorted, demented. I pulled out; the girl, safely away, only a memory. As I weaved through traffic, I struggled to keep control of the car. I was trembling at the thought of what I had almost done, what I'd become.

I wasn't like them. I'd never known this urge before.

What if the girl had not run away? And what if she had gotten into my car?

How far would I have gone? In a few minutes I went from being horror-struck to fantasizing about having her next to me. About driving to some unknown destination. About some old mill, maybe?

Jesus, how could these thoughts ever enter *my* head?

I wasn't my father, my grandfather. I couldn't bear the thought of harming another human being, let alone a little girl.

But what would happen if she did go with me?

Would she keep our encounter quiet, or would she tell? God, if she told anyone, I would lose everything— my job, our home, you. I couldn't stand the thought of losing you.

No, if she was going to tell someone, well, I would have had to find a way to silence her.

Silence her?

She's a little girl, for Christ's sake. Of course she'll talk.

You have to know that going in.

You'd have to know it the minute you pulled up.

You'd have to be committed to silencing her from the start.

I had to pull over before I hit something. My own thoughts were driving me mad. I kept telling myself I was a good person. I wouldn't hurt her. But the truth was, I knew: if she had gotten into my car, she would never see her family again. I knew that if she had come with me, my mind would lock her away in the same cell as the girl in the brown sundress.

And as horrible as this was, my little man, there was a piece of me that thought it might have been . . . acceptable.

I know it's crazy; I hadn't been around those men for twenty-five years. They had no more power over me. So what in God's name made me do what I'd just done?

If I was going to find out, I realized, I was going to have to go to the source. I was going to have to return to the farm.

I STILL HAD A PRETTY good idea where the place was. Google Earth helped me locate it fairly quickly. It was desolate, son. Always had been. Perfect for the type of activities they were involved in.

The road up to the house was almost a mile long. Tree-lined, it sheltered their lair from the outside world. Just off the highway that led to the city where I first met Henry and Mary, the farm was surprisingly close to civilization, yet completely isolated.

It was no more than a five- or six-hour drive from where I had settled with Suzane; for two days I prepared for my return.

Did I have a plan?

Not exactly—but as with my escape, I had a rough outline.

Did I know I was going to kill them?

Not really.

Was it out of the question?

No.

Anyway, it's all of this that brought us here, now, to this old table. It's why I'm writing this letter, explaining to my only son what I've done.

And you know what it all boils down to? I did what had to be done. Son, that's really all there is to it.

I PACKED THE CAR early this morning and we hit the road, you and I. You were full of questions.

"Where are we going? Look at that big truck! Why are we going? What's that?"

The world is a wondrous thing in the eyes of a child.

Did you experience the same awe I felt on my first big road trip? You slept a little, but more often than not you were a great co-pilot. Maybe you wouldn't have been if you knew who we were looking for.

I was nervous and I'm sure it was obvious. You kept asking, "What's wrong?" Kids are intuitive. . . . Whenever I felt like turning back, I would look over at you. And I knew that I had to keep driving.

I have to say—you're so beautiful, so innocent, that it was tough to keep my mind on the road. Maybe it's because you look so much like your mother; maybe it's just because you're you.

About an hour before we were going to arrive, I stopped and gave you some dinner. I wanted to be sure you weren't awake to witness this, so I added something to your juice to help you sleep.

You complained about the taste, but you drank anyway. We headed back out on the road and you fell asleep quickly. Before you did you reached across the seat to me and said, "I love you, Daddy."

I can't explain to you what that meant to me, son. Fighting another lump I grabbed your hand and said, "I love you, too, little man."

And I do, son. More that anything. I would protect you from anything. I would give my life for you.

It was early in the evening when we got to the long driveway. There was a gate, a rusty lock and a fading sign that read, "No Trespassing."

I came prepared. I got out of the car and went to the trunk for the bolt cutters and the gun. With the lock cut and the sawed-off on my lap, I drove the longest mile, blinking to keep focus.

Part of me, sure, wanted to turn around and pretend none of it had happened. But I'd gone too far. Nothing could prevent what was going to happen from happening—there was no safety net under this high-wire.

The sun was just setting on the farmhouse and the empty lot where the old mill had stood so many years before.

The house was in utter disrepair. In the last light, the windows seemed to shine like an evil neon. There was no sign of life—and I think I feared they were both dead, that I would never get the answers I needed. I also had enough anger in my heart to understand that if they were dead, I wanted to be a part of the glorious process.

I didn't hate them for what they had done to me, son, but for what they'd passed on to me. And a part of me hated them, too, for not killing me when they had the chance.

I pulled the car up and waited for one or both of them to appear.

It was only a few moments before the old wooden door swung inward. A barely recognizable old man in a wheelchair was pushed onto the porch by an equally changed old man.

My grandfather had aged significantly in the two

and a half decades since the truck fell onto him. He looked to be in his eighties and sat almost motionless, a blanket covering his lap.

The anger in his eyes was made impotent by the haggardness of his face. I could see that he desperately wanted to get up and teach a lesson to whoever the trespasser was. His body, however, was never going to allow it to happen. Time, son, time is the great equalizer. I hoped his last years had been as miserable as he appeared to be.

The old man behind him? The yellow-green eyes confirmed what a lack of hair and his frailty could not: this was my father.

No longer a powerful, drunken, forty-year-old bully, he'd become a pathetic, slouching, sixty-something has-been.

They waited, both staring at the car.

I covered you with a blanket, son. They were not good enough to lay eyes on someone so fine.

I got out, shotgun under my coat, and stood with just the air between them and me. I didn't say a word; I wanted them to do the talking, wanted to know if they could figure out who I was—and why I was there.

The old man spoke, barely audible: "How the fuck you get in here?"

I didn't answer.

My father stepped from behind the wheelchair. "He said, 'How the fuck you get in here?' Cain't you read? Sign says no trespassing."

I don't know where the courage came from, but I smiled.

"The fuck you want? And whatta you smiling at?"

I rubbed the side of my face where, many years earlier, my father had burned hope into me.

He squinted to get a better look, then shook his head in disbelief and stepped back to whisper something to the old man.

"Whatta ya mean, he's back?"

Louder now, not taking his eyes off me, my father leaned in again and told my grandfather that I had returned to the farm. From his wheelchair the old man mouthed "Mother*fucker.*"

My father, straightening himself to look stronger, adjusted his belt and glared.

The old man looked simply confused.

"What the fuck you want, boy?" my father asked.

I hadn't been called "boy" in a long time. I didn't know enough back then to be insulted.

"The name is Tom," I said.

"Tom?" the old man said.

"Tom?" My father spat.

"Yes, Tom." I was assertive, but calm.

"Whatever. You got no business here, *Tom*. You ran away. Remember? We weren't good enough for you. So get the fuck out afore I give you another beating."

My father's fists were clenched. He was hoping I'd

back down just like I had so many times before. He was in no shape to give anyone a beating, and he knew it.

"You're wrong. I'm not going anywhere and I've got lots of business here. Unfinished business."

The old man sat nodding in his wheelchair, and I actually think he was mildly amused. He wouldn't be for long.

"I've got some questions for you, *father*."

"Questions? What kinda questions?"

"You already know. And you're going to answer me. I want to know how a father keeps his own son hostage, living like a slave. How he allows his own father to beat the shit out of his flesh and blood." I was on the verge of yelling, finger on the trigger of the shotgun under my coat. It's amazing I hadn't already pulled the trigger.

"Slave. Jeezus. You hear that, Pa? Boy says we kept him like a slave. Ya hear that? Fool came way out here to know why we beat him. Boy, you are 'bout as dumb as the day you left. Shitferbrains." He spat again.

"You don't know why we beat you? You don't, do ya? Fuck me. You were and still are one useless piece a shit. Only thing you understood was my boot in yer ribs. Slavery? We fuckin' fed you, gave you a bed; what else you deserve? Fucking crawlspace was too good—and don't think I didn't know you was stealing vegetables. I knew it the whole time. 'Course, I never told Pa—he'd a wanted to kick the shit outta ya. I didn't give a fuck.

166

If you was too hurt you was no good to no one. No, boy, I fuckin' protected you. The only reason you was able to leave was because I let you, boy."

"You got one thing right," I said. "You helped me escape. Of course you have no idea how. But I do owe it all to you."

He looked puzzled, then mumbled, "That it, boy? Okay, we beat you. That what you want to hear? You said your piece. Now fuck off."

It was clear he wasn't sure why I was really there, and it was also clear he didn't really want to know.

"And what about the girls?"

I said it before I could think it through properly.

"Girls?"

"The girls. The girls you and the old man took to the mill. What about them?"

"Whatta ya mean whattabout them?"

"You know goddamned well what I mean." My father was finally staring into his own rage-filled yellow-green eyes—and he was scared.

He shifted his weight and leaned on the porch post.

"Why did you do it? How many were there?"

"Why? Where you goin' with this, boy? Just where the fuck you goin'?"

Then the old man moved the blanket and revealed the small gun he'd had nestled on his lap.

I saw the muzzle flash and heard the bullet whiz

past my head as I dove behind the car's fender.

I had never fired a gun before—but this was the perfect time to try.

I moved behind the car and leaned across the trunk while they were still focused on the front.

I aimed the shotgun at them, not fifteen feet from me, pulled the trigger and hoped for the best.

The kick of the recoil knocked me to the ground. I lay on my back there a second, dazed from the sound the thing made.

"Jeezus, Pa, he got you. Oh fuck, Pa, where's the gun? Jeezus fuck, he's killed you."

I knew I was safe. My father was hysterical, still scrambling to find the gun.

"Just stop," I said.

The old man had been blown out of the chair. He was lying on his side, clutching at his stomach, moving his bloodied lips, but saying nothing.

"You motherfucker, you shot my pa." His green-yellow eyes were wild, not with anger, but with fear. He had every reason to be scared. I had just blown a fist-sized hole in my grandfather and didn't feel one ounce of regret. In fact, it felt pretty damn good.

"What's wrong with you? You just shot your grandfather. Ain't you got no sense of decency?"

"Who are you to use that word with me? That man lying there is not my real grandfather. And you are not my real father. My real father was a good man, and he died a long time ago. You aren't a tenth of the man he was, so don't go preaching decency to me."

He was shaking; he knew, as I did, that I wasn't done. For a second, I swear, his eyes became as soft as they had on the night he burned me—when he was laughing, play-acting, showing me the paper money.

"Son, hold on a minute. It weren't me. It was the old man. It was always the old man."

He stood, hands outstretched, pleading for understanding. But the time for understanding, son, had long passed. There he was, placing all of the blame on his dying father.

You know, son, they say a gut shot is the most painful way to go.

I only hope that's true.

"Son? Tom, is it? Listen. Tom, you asked about the girls and I'll tell ya. Put that gun away, an' I'll tell ya. Honest, I got nothing to hide. Really, Tom. Just point that thing away."

I lowered the gun to my side.

We stood just five feet apart now, both of us on the porch, watching the old man take his last breath.

"Whatta ya need to know, Tom? I don't wanna go like that," he said, pointing at his dead father.

Darkness was taking over; I told him to turn on a light. I followed him as he reached inside the door and grabbed the lantern.

I could see him clearly now. His face was like old

leather, taut but lined. He'd taken on that skeletal form of most lifelong farmers, lean, hard, broken.

I think he was starting to see how much I resembled him.

"Tell me why. I just want to know why?"

"It was the old man. Always the old man. He'd go to town and more often than not bring one back. He loved the young ones. Always did."

"What about you? You just let it happen."

"What could I do? You know what a mean sonofabitch he was."

He was actually trying to charm me now.

"Look, Tom, I couldn't have stopped him even if I tried."

"But you didn't try, did you?"

"Honestly? No. But at the end I always made sure they didn't suffer none."

"At the end? At the end? What does that mean?" I pointed the barrel right at his chest.

"Easy, Tom." He stepped back. "Easy. You know when we . . . when *he* was done with them . . . I made it real quick. . . ."

"You said *we.* You were just as guilty, weren't you?"

He stood focused on the gun.

"Say it, you son of a bitch, or I'll open you up just like him."

"Okay, okay. Maybe I used them too. But I couldn't

help it." Tears began rolling down his cracked cheeks. "I couldn't stop myself. I had to have 'em. I mean, yer grandpa'd bring 'em home and they was so young and pretty and soft . . . I just couldn't help it. They was here anyways, right? They was gonna die anyways. So I might as well . . ."

I'd heard enough. "Had to have 'em" echoed around in my head while memories of two days earlier came rushing back and fractured. Images fell like ash—into the broken fingernails at the base of the column in the old mill.

I was going to be sick, and staggered from the truth: just like my father, I had to have them, too.

Seeing his opportunity, my father lunged. I had just enough strength to pull the trigger as he landed on me.

We were face to face when the slug tore him apart. His eyes went blank: there was no more green-yellow rage left.

I shoved him off but lay there, trying to get my bearings.

I had just killed two men. I had killed my grandfather and my father, and I had no regrets. The two most evil men in my world were gone, burning in whatever hell whatever God they believed in had consigned them to.

I hope there are rats there. Big ones.

I got up and stared at them, cold and dead. Oddly,

maybe, I felt nothing, no release or real emotion. I wasn't appalled. I wasn't repulsed by the condition of their bodies. I felt nothing.

I walked back to the car where you were still sleeping, picked you up, blanket and all, and carried you over the bodies of your ancestors. I carried you into the house where I was enslaved as a child, and put you where you are lying now.

It's been some time now, since I started writing. I pumped up the oil lamp, out of habit, the way that I did when I was a boy out here. The lamp wants to rest, but the last of its oil burns so I can finish this for you. It's almost daybreak, son, and you see, I grow weary. I want to join you in rest, but I can't just yet—there's more to say.

I walked over to you several times while writing this, little man, just checking on you. Why wouldn't you be safe? I had just killed two of the most dangerous men in your world; what else could threaten you?

I'll try to explain.

For two days, I've thought endlessly about what I did to that little girl. The truth's been right there, staring me in the face, but I didn't want to see it. Think of it this way, son: imagine knowing you've got a terminal disease but refusing to see a doctor because he'll confirm it. . . .

Tonight, my father confirmed my self-diagnosis. I have an illness. A cancer passed from my grandfather to my father and from my father to me.

I had to rid us all of this illness, son, before anyone else was consumed. I had no choice. I hope you can forgive me.

A few moments ago I walked over, picked you up and held you in my arms. I stared at your cherubic face, still round with baby fat, so wondrous, so pure. Did we all begin so innocently? Did evil metastasize to make us so grotesque, so monstrous? Would our mothers, as they nursed us, if they knew . . . would they have done the right thing? How many mothers look back at the evil done by sons they've raised and wish their child had never been born? Would they have had the courage to stop the disease before it ever spread?

Son, I don't know.

But while I held you, I know I looked at you, curly-haired, soft and beautiful, and I cried as your breath became shallower. With each moment I held you they became further apart. And then son, finally, you gasped your last breath, and joined your mother in heaven.

You were the last link in the chain, little man. The culmination of this genetic nightmare. I could not risk passing this on to you.

You are the most important thing in my life and I have to protect you.

I have to protect you from you.

I'm having trouble writing now, son. My vision is

blurred with these tears and my mind is fogged by the same drugs I gave you. It won't be long now. Hopefully I'll begin my journey to you and your mother soon.

When they find us later today, I will be holding you. We're on the old wooden chair. My letter to you is beside us on the table.

I mentioned, earlier, my preparations. Part of that was writing another letter, directions included, to the local police. They will understand why I've done what I've done, I think. And hopefully someone will explain it to Mary.

I can't wait to hold you in my arms once more.

I love you, little man.

— Dad

xo xo

ACKNOWLEDGMENTS

Laura Hobbs and Krystal Tobias: in memorium, 2005.

Thanks to my wife, Suzane, for putting up with my odd, difficult behavior—and for letting me be me. You keep me grounded and on the right path. To my children, Angèle and Eric, thank you for understanding that sometimes Daddy just needed to be left alone to put his thoughts on paper.

Thanks to Jon and Jeff, two special people whose faith, encouragement and friendship have given me the confidence to write this. It never would have happened without your support.

Thanks to Ginette, for making *Hope Burned* a part of her always busy schedule.

Thanks to Michael, my editor, my friend. This journey has been made even more special because of your encouraging and gentle guidance. We will take many more trips together; let's hope they are just as interesting and enjoyable.

Lastly, thanks to anyone who might be reading my first novel. It's an honor, whenever someone allows you into their world. Thank you for inviting me into yours.